The Nightlife Chronicles

The Nightlife Chronicles

Shawn Flossy

Shawn Flossy

SBN-10: 0-9975851-0-2
ISBN-13: 978-0-9975851-0-0

First printing
Printed in the United States

Published by PURP Publications

Be infinitely motivated to do the things that others say you cannot.

Scorching Summer

1 The Pleasure is All Mine

I wanted to fuck his dick off from the moment I saw him. Tall and chocolate, just like I like 'em. But I couldn't. I have a serious thing for super attractive candy bar like men, but I like to think I'm a woman with morals, or what not, so, I do my best not to talk to off the market men. One of the girls from the office, Ty, was surprised when her boyfriend came in this afternoon to bring her some lunch. This was the first time she introduced us to her significant other and I could see why. I would keep him to myself too. His demeanor was mysterious yet sexy and even though he made no immediate remarks or actions I could tell he was checking me out. Guys always give off that vibe when they wouldn't mind fucking you.

"Rodney, Taya. Taya, Rodney," Ty introduced us. She spoke nonchalantly, not knowing I was plotting on her man.

"Nice to meet you." He extended his arm. His firm grip sent chills up my spine as I embraced his gesture.

"The pleasure is all mine," I reacted to his statement. I smiled then turned around and went back into my office.

They left and I watched him walk toward the elevators through the glass walls of my office. His walk was commanding, demanding all my attention as if he knew I was watching him. And for a quick second I had the sexual fantasy of him thrusting in and out of me up against my desk in the middle of the day, then I came back to reality, realizing that he was taken and I personally don't care for leftovers. Though, I would devour every bit of his manhood.

I was swamped that day. I had an Executive Board meeting on Monday that I wasn't nearly prepared for and four projects just waiting to be finished. So, I stayed late wrapping things up. My secretary made every attempt to keep me rejuvenated, dropping off can after can of Red Bull and making periodic snack breaks. Though I dread nights like this, I absolutely love my job. As a Marketing Vice President for a top Fortune 500 company I have very little to complain about financially.

After four years of undergrad and two years of graduate school I can admit that every homework assignment, class lecture, and group project was worth it. It took me a while to figure it out, but I did the work and I must say it pays off. I make well over six figures, live in a luxury apartment, and drive a brand new Range Rover and a drop top BMW on the weekends. And that's just a few of my expenses. I spend a good portion on physical maintenance, such as hair and wardrobe, despite the fact that I make looking this good look easy. I also spend quite a bit sending money back home to my parents in Tallahassee, but I wouldn't dare complain for one second about it.

My father worked seventy-hour workweeks and my mother pushed two jobs just to fund my entire undergrad experience. I gladly pay to ensure that they don't ever have to lift another finger. I even return the favor by sponsoring my baby sister through beauty school. Though I spend lots of money on those things, I have to admit that majority of my funds go towards my Nightlife experiences. Between the bottles at the clubs and the last minute flights to Vegas I could probably feed an entire third world village.

I would love to say that my behavior today in the office is outside of my norm, but the truth is, it isn't unusual for me to fantasize about sexually appealing men throughout the day, seeing that I'm going through a bit of a dry spell. I haven't been in a committed relationship for over a year now. And thanks to my ex, Sly, I don't think I ever want to be called someone's "girl" again. Sly was just one of those guys that every woman has to run across who teaches them about men. About the low down dirty game and how they will run through countless amounts of women tearing their hearts into pieces until they find the right woman for them. Sly taught me a lot about putting too much effort in too early.

After I wrapped up my evening I took the first opportunity to get out of my office and clear my mind from my job. Once I got back to my apartment I hopped in the shower and got fresh for The Nightlife. The Nightlife is my everyday escape from my monotonous corporate life. I come alive at night and turn my personality all the way up. The Nightlife is my excuse to practice the art of playing men. And I must admit that I'm not a pro yet. Unfortunately, being a "player" is unnatural for us women. Women love the concreteness of having one man who is completely wrapped up into them, but in reality we have to deal with the immature process that every man has to go through.

Tonight, I'm dressed modestly: a red body glove cocktail dress that barely came past my cheeks, nude Louboutin pumps, and my hair was bone straight down my back. I hopped in my dynamic driving machine and drove downtown to meet up with my girls at Jasmine's Night Club.

Jasmine's Night Club is one of the hottest spots to hit on a Friday night. On the outside, the venue looks super clean and simple, almost like a fancy restaurant, but once you get inside things tend to get wild. I pulled up in the front and allowed the valet to take my car. I stepped toward the club entrance and all eyes were on me, as they should be. On my way in, I noticed how packed it was. It was barely ten minutes after midnight and the general admission line was wrapped around the corner. I skipped the line and went in through the VIP entrance. An acquaintance of mine manages the club and has me on the VIP forever list. When I got inside I immediately hit the bar and demanded a margarita. I tip nicely so the bartenders always show love.

After I grabbed my drink, I quickly scanned the room and found my girls at a table near the dance floor. I licked my lips, flipped my hair, and let my ass bounce behind me as I made my way to our table. I took amusement from watching men drool over my body that was wrapped tightly by this red dress.

"Damn how'd y'all get this clutch ass table?" I asked noticing the perfect location to where we were sitting.

"We got here early so we don't have to deal with that long ass line! Everybody's not on the VIP list like you,"

Camille yelled over the loud music.

I nodded in agreement.

"Taya is that the dress we saw last weekend?" Angela snapped at me. "I thought you said you weren't going to buy it."

"Is it a problem that I did, Angela?" I snapped back.

"You know I was thinking about buying that dress!" she peered her eyes at me.

"See that's the difference between me and you. You think and I take action!" Angela rolled her eyes.

Angela is one of my homegirls but I keep her at a distance. She's an Advertising Director for Axium and Co., a software company very similar to my firm; we met at a networking event a few years back over cocktails (I make a lot of my friends that way) and she introduced herself to me thinking I was at the same level as her. She also thought it was appropriate to draw the "black card" stating "It's hard for sisters like us to make it to the VP and President positions". When she looked over to me for my gesture of approval and noticed I wasn't laughing she immediately knew she fucked up.

I thought her reaction was funny and laughed and took a sip of my drink then simply told her, "I agree it's hard, but when you're a boss people tend to take notice."

After she let the bitterness of our conversation go she made the right move in further enhancing our relationship and I accepted because, quite frankly, I liked her honesty. Ever since that day we been kicking it during The Nightlife despite the fact that she likes to throw shade from time to time. I'm not exactly sure why but I think it's because she secretly wants to be like me. I always say you have to have that one friend around that hates on you just a little bit, that way you know you still got it.

"Anyway. What's good? Is it poppin' in here or do we need to move around?" I asked my girls.

"Naw, we good here. I spotted plenty of "potential" already!" Camille blurted out.

Now Camille, on the other hand, is my ride or die. We've been down with each other since way back. Running the streets and playing these niggas were our hobbies. Camille is a bartender at a strip club downtown by night while she works on her medical degree by day. She is my sexy "wing-man" homegirl that keeps me on my toes. She's cute, petite with a slim waist but that ass is fat. And to compliment her banging body she has a pretty face, dimples, and a bubbly personality.

I met Camille in high school. We both were the stuck up type, acting like we were too good to introduce ourselves to one another. That all changed when some bony bitch with glasses and nappy edges thought she was gone clown on everybody in our class. Camille and I took turns clowning that bitch until our teacher finished writing our insubordination notices and sent us to the office. We bonded in the Principal's office and found out that we had a lot of similarities. Ever since then we been kicking it.

I took notice to the atmosphere. The club was packed tight. Plenty of bop bitches looking to get chose and just as many dusty dudes ready to take them home and use them. I noticed the bougie hoes in the building. These females were much like me and my clique except a lot of them were fake bougie trying extra hard just to keep up. Those type women don't come to the club for the men. They come out to hate. They see a bitch like me that is unbothered and they try their best to find a flaw. Unfortunately for them, ain't no flaws bitch.

Just as I was finishing my room scan Ty's fine ass boyfriend, Rodney, walked past our table. What a coincidence. Earlier today I was thinking about test driving him and here he comes pulling up right in front of me with the keys in the ignition.

"Oh my fuckin goodness," I spoke as I tapped Camille on her leg. "Did you see that fine ass chocolate man that just passed?"

"Hell yea I saw him!!"

"I met him earlier, his girl works in my office."

"Oh really..." Camille remarked as she seductively sipped her cocktail.

"Yea. She brought him in this afternoon. I peeped his fine ass then."

"Are you gon hop on that or do I need to do it?" Camille stated and she was not playing.

"Camille, I just said he had a girl!!"

"So! Niggas don't give a fuck about that shit. I bet money he would let you fuck. So get yo ass up and go get that shit."

I pondered that scandalous ass offer as I downed my Patron margarita, and then I got my fine ass up and walked toward the dance floor. It was easy to spot Rodney; he had to be at least six-feet five. I walked up to him, looked at him dead in his eyes then I turned around and threw it back at him. He immediately embraced my curves with his big strong hands. As the song played he caressed my body, he was turning me all the way on. The song switched over to a slow jam giving him the opportunity to fully embrace me. I turned rested my ass up against his manhood and slowly danced to the beat and he rested his head on my shoulder as he whispered, "You were looking so damn good earlier."

"Oh, so you remember me," I smiled.

"Hell yea, who could forget Taya?"

I was flattered that he remembered me. He made resisting him a lot harder than I initially thought it would be. *Should I try him out and deal with the consequences of his girlfriend later? Or pass him up and pick a different victim for tonight?*

I turned around, facing him, then I asked the question that we were both thinking.
"So, what's next?"

Rodney gave me that look like he was definitely down. I quickly made my way over to our table and grabbed my purse.

"I got action," I said to my girls with a wink. They shrilled and start immediately gossiping.

"I told you so!" Camille yelled across the room as I made my way back to Rodney.

I had barely been in this club for a whole hour and here I am ready to ruin this man's relationship. I gave him the address to my apartment complex then I got in the car and whipped down the highway to my crib. Thirty minutes later I was ridin' his dick like I was a professional jockey on my California king mattress.

My ass bounced up and down as I held his hands back against the bed. His moans got louder and louder and he refused to stop screaming my name. Forty-five seconds later his eyes rolled into the back of his head and his meat went completely limp. He busted, filling the condom. I hopped off him and angrily threw the covers over my bare body and within the next few seconds that nigga was snoring.

2 Pink Bikini

I almost forgot about the wack dick I had the night before until I rolled over and saw Rodney drooling on my satin pillow. The nerve of this nigga, in my bed snoring with his crusty toes balled up against my leg after he weak stroked me last night.

"Rodney!!" I screamed and hit him over the head with a pillow. "Get yo ass up!"

He squinted his eyes, barely opening them.

"Girl, why you trippin?" He said abruptly as he wiped the drool from his chin. His morning breath damn near burned a hole in my expensive sheets.

"You gotta go, I got things to do today."

I lied. I had absolutely nothing to do today. But he damn sure wasn't bout to lay up in my bed until noon. Hell no. I rudely helped expedite his waking up process by throwing his clothes at him as he dragged himself out of the bed. He didn't even have both shoes on before I was standing at the door motioning for him to get the fuck out!

"So I'ma call you later—" I closed the door in his face before he could even finish.

After Rodney left, I showered and wiped the stench of "ain't shit nigga" off my beautiful brown skin. I threw on a tan summer halter dress and flopped on the couch. I'm normally lazy on Saturday morning but since I had to get up early to get rid of unwanted guests I can start my day a little earlier. I needed to find a move, quickly. So, I called my girl, Camille.

"Camille, what's up?"

"What's good Taya!!" She responded anxiously. "We hitting up this pool party today girl, supposed to be popping from what I heard." She immediately knew why I called.

"Well, shit I'm down for whatever! When you coming to scoop me?"

"I'll be there around noon, don't have me waiting outside either!'

I hung up the phone with Camille and instantly started rummaging through my closet for my swimsuits. My walk-in closet never allows me to find anything efficiently. Though there is plenty of space the amount of clothes, shoes, accessories and handbags I have just screams chaos. I pulled out this tight hot pink bikini, black Balenciaga wedges, and my Louis Vuitton shades to complete the fit. I knew that a pool party meant an opportunity to stunt, which is something I don't pass up often.

Camille and I pulled up to this modest sized mansion in the south suburbs. We were in full blown out laughter over the whole Rodney situation as we parked.

"But he looked like he had so much potential," Camille managed to get out in the midst of her hysterical laughter.

"Potential my ass," I said in an extremely sarcastic voice. "Young "Pump" Daddy was not about to Make the Band with that baby ass stroke game," I clowned. Camille screamed laughing at my puns and added fuel to the fire.

"Let's just focus on this new action we're bouta get into. Whose party is this?"

"Some nigga named Mike," Camille shrugged as if it didn't matter.

"Some nigga?" I questioned.

"Yea, some nigga. I don't really know the dude. Does it even matter?"

"I mean no, it doesn't matter. I'm just trying to figure out how you find out about stuff like this and you don't even know the guy."

"I'm connected. What can I say?"

Camille was right; she is connected. She probably knows more celebrities than I do. She not only knows them but interacts with them on a regular basis. When Snoop comes into town he personally calls her to join his "sessions" at his hotel. And when Erykah Badu comes to perform at the local poetry spots she crashes at Camille's apartment.

We got out of Camille's white Honda Accord and crossed the street to the house. Camille was rockin a fresh ass classic black bikini with some new tan wedges straight out of Aldo. We walked up a massive driveway passing by a brand new red Dodge Charger and a charcoal grey CL550 Mercedes-Benz Coup. As we approached the back gate to the pool entrance we realized how deep this party was. Camille and I love to be the center of attention and as we walked through the thick crowd that was exactly what we were, all eyes were on us. I couldn't help but to smirk as I watched other females turn their nose up at me as their boyfriends plotted on how they would approach me. Ha!

"Hey, Shorty. What's yo name?"

"Damn, what's yo number?"

"Ay. Pink Bikini!"

Of course, I ignored all those middle school ass pick

up lines.

"Where all the fine men at though, with that bankroll?" Camille asked.

"I have yet to see one, it ain't nothin but broke ass thugs in this bitch," I replied.

After I grabbed one of the complimentary cocktails, I copped a seat at the bar and scanned the scene. For the most part this was your typical summer pool party. Lots of pretty females walking around half naked and males running their best game to land them some pussy before the day is over. I looked over toward the patio door into the house and saw a group of men circled up having every day convo, from what I could tell. I recognized a few of them, one of the guys Camille knows from the bar and a guy from my gym. They were way too far away to tell but, it looked as if they were the "it" group of the party. They were probably the owner's friends or the party promoters.

Camille and I dipped in the pool for a few minutes then got back out. I didn't want to risk the chance of somebody splashing water on me and fucking up my hair. I know that's very "typical black girl" of me but, my hair is a bitch to straighten and I just don't have the time for it today. While I was drying off this handsome ass chocolate skinned, six-feet three brother walked directly up to me.

"Every nigga in this party asking me about some fine brown skinned chick with a hot pink bikini on. That must be you." He smiled. I laughed. "What's good, I'm Money Mike." he said as he extended his hand for a handshake.

I received his hand. "I'm Taya. Nice to meet you." I said in the most flirtatious voice I could muster up.

"Taya. That's sexy, just like you." And then he smiled and all I could do was melt on the inside. Pearly white teeth and dimples are always a plus in my book.

"I'm flattered," I stated modestly.

He stared directly into my eyes and handed me his iPhone. I took his phone out of his hand and then he looked off as if he was waiting for me to finish a task. He didn't even say a word. His confidence was such a turn on. I put my number in his phone and saved it under Taya with a wink emoji behind it. I handed his phone back to him and before I could even say anything some random ass chick bombarded her way between us. She literally pushed up against me to create space between Mike and I.

"Who the fuck is you?" She rudely blurted out with her tacky improper grammar.

"Naw, Who the fuck are you?" I snapped back without even thinking.

"This is my nigga that yo weak ass is drooling all over!"

"Damn, his bad! It ain't my fault he tryna upgrade!"

"Bitch fuck you!!

"Naw, bitch! I'ma fuck him!" I said as I pointed at Mike. I only said that to piss her off. I wasn't actually planning on fucking him, yet.

"Aw hell naw..." she yelled as Mike grabbed her up by her shirt.

"Ashley chill, damn! How the fuck yo ass even get in here? I told you not to bring yo ratchet ass to my house no more." He went off on her as he escorted her in the house.

I turned around and Camille was standing directly behind me, ready to fight. "That bitch ain't want it with you, Taya, trust me. She woulda had four fists coming at her like clockwork."

I wasn't even tripping; I live for an adrenaline rush like that! We laughed at the altercation as we continued to mingle. The encounter with Ashley became a distant memory. Camille got five numbers, one from this fine educated Jamaican brother who seemed to be really interested in her. I got a few more numbers, but I couldn't stop thinking about Mike's pretty ass smile. I didn't see him anymore after the altercation. He probably was embarrassed.

A few hours later, Camille and I hopped in the Accord and headed back to our side of town.

3 The Pool Party

I spend most of my day on the phone cursing muthafuckas out.

"Bitch, I told you I needed all my bread by Friday. It's Saturday!"

"Man, Money Mike, my bad bro. I had been meaning to stop by yo office all day! I swear."

"Miss me with all the bullshit my nigga and just bring me my cash."

Like I was saying, I spend most of my day cursing people out. It's a part of the industry. I'm a self-proclaimed baller and I got the bank accounts to prove it. I own my own studio in downtown Miami; my office sits on the top floor. Most of my revenue comes from selling studio time slots. I make extra cash with my events. I host and promote all the livest parties in the city. Ask anybody, they know me.

After I hung the phone up with Ja, an owner of a club where I hosted a party at last week, I turned around and hit my boy Dre. "What's good, Money Mike?"

"Shit, bouta leave the office and head to the pool party. What it's looking like?"

I always host a pool party at my crib on the first Saturday of each month during the summer. I'm talking nothing but the finest females, big time celebrities, and businessmen are invited. And just to make sure I have the place swarming with attractive women I insisted every woman brings at least one bad chick. I got people calling me now just to get on the VIP list for next summer.

"This hoe rocking! Ain't nothing but thick hoes in this bitch."

"Sounds about right, on my way!"

I got a fat ass crib in the south suburbs, sitting on a hill secluded from the neighborhood. All there is in my neighborhood are rich lawyers and doctors and their wives stay staring at me like a young nigga don't belong. I don't give a fuck though. The fact that I came straight from the hood and built my own multimillion dollar empire without going to college just makes me five times tighter than any doctor or lawyer. I rode up the street to my house passing hundreds of cars. When I got to the driveway I swooped in and parked my decked out charcoal grey CL550.

I walked in the front door and my crib was covered with fine ass females in bikinis. I love females, what nigga wouldn't. The thing about me is, I can spot a gold-digger a mile away and I cannot stand a broke bitch, so it's hard for me to find a shorty that I would actually wife. But when it comes to fucking these hoes, it's no problem at all. I spotted Dre on the couch surrounded by a few.

"What's good, Bro?" I dapped Dre.

"Hey, ladies," I said suavely.

"Hey, Mike!" they sounded off in unison.

Layla, one of the chicks that I'm known for fucking with from time to time, walks up to me and cuffs her arm on mine. This girl swears up and down she gone be my wifey one day. I just can't do it though, for two reasons. Reason number one: she's a receptionist at a dentist's office. Which, to me, means that she looking for a way to quick success. Don't get me wrong, I understand that everyone has to start somewhere to build their way up. But, shorty is damn near thirty and has had the same job for eight years. She ain't ambitious enough for me. I just can't get with that. Reason number two: she smashed the homie. Enough said. Me and my boys don't mind passing these hoes, we actually do that shit all the time. But, I refuse to wife a hoe that has smashed one or many of my immediate homies. I ain't the one.

"Mikey when you gone take me out to dinner?" The

bitch had the nerve to ask.

"Dinner? I'll take you up to my room and I can put this meat in yo mouth. If that's what you meant," I replied as I removed her arm.

Dre busted straight out laughing. "You wild, boy!"

Layla walked off with an attitude, like I gave a fuck. I stepped to the sliding glass door that opened up to the backyard patio. I'm talking bout it was so many people, my shit looked like a Birdman music video. I scanned the area and most of the people looked familiar except for a few people. But this one chick in particular caught my eye. She was standing with a chick in a black bikini and she was in a pink one. Shorty in the pink bikini was bad from head to toe. She looked like she was about five-feet nine with heels on, pretty ass smooth brown skin, long black hair and she had this confident ass swag about her.

"Dre! Come here."

Dre got up and came to the glass door with me. "What's up?"

"You see that chick in the pink bikini right here, who is she?" I asked as I pointed her out.

"Shit, I don't know. I know the girl she with though, that's Camille. She used to be a bartender at Exposure."

"You hit that?" I mannishly asked. I was slightly familiar with Camille; saw her at exposure once or twice.

"Naw, bro, but I wish."

I walked outside while Dre was still reminiscing. The thing about me is that I don't have an ounce of shyness in my blood. When I want something I go get it, period.

On my way over to her I noticed a lot of niggas trying to get at her and she was turning them down. That made me even more intrigued with her. After a while she saw me walking up to her. I knew I was swaggin' so I wasn't worried. I was stunting in some classic Trues with the white stitching, Damier Louis belt, and Polo V-neck. I was on some basic shit but fresh as fuck nonetheless. I was licking my lips as I checked out her frame. Her *pillows* were sitting up right, probably a D cup from what I could tell. And that ass was poking out from the front.

Once I got close enough I dropped a line on her. "So, you must be the gorgeous chick in the pink bikini that all my boys keep asking about." I lied; nobody had asked me about her.

She laughed. "Must be me."

"What I'm tryna figure out is how you at my crib and I haven't had the pleasure of meeting you?"

"Oh, so this is your party?"

I extended my hand. "I'm Money Mike."

She accepted my greeting. "Taya, pleasure to meet you."

"The pleasure is all mine."

I could tell I won her over already. She was straight going for ya boy. So, I pulled my iPhone out my pocket and handed it to her. I didn't say shit; she knew what was up. She put her number in my phone and handed it back.

"You gone call me?" She curiously asked.

"You will see," I said and then I winked at her.

Right when I was about to open the convo up some more my ex, Ashley, walked her jealous ass right between us.

"Who the fuck is you?" She rudely blurted out.

"Naw, who the fuck are you!?" Taya bucked back.

"This is my nigga that yo weak ass is drooling all over!"

"Damn, his bad! It ain't my fault he tryna upgrade!"

I was cracking up on the inside.

"Bitch fuck you!!" Ashley yelled.

"Naw, bitch! I'ma fuck him!" Taya said as she pointed at me with an eager look on her face.

"Aw hell naw..." Ashley yelled.

I grabbed the girl up by her shirt. "Ashley chill, damn! How the fuck yo ass even get in here? I told you not to bring yo ratchet ass to my house no more."

I went off then escorted Ashley through the house and out the front door. I made sure she got in her car and drove off. I swear that's one of the things about my life that I don't personally prefer. The fact that I get so many women and then when I cut them off, they go crazy. And much like Ashley, most of them try to sneak their way back inside.

That bitch fucked my whole game up. I was planning on smooth talking Taya right into my bed that night but, things didn't turn out that way. It's all good though I have a feeling I'll redeem myself. I went back in the house to the kitchen and made myself a drink, Henny on the rocks. I copped a seat on my couch between some thick hoes and continued to enjoy myself.

From my couch, I peeped Taya through the glass door getting major play from every nigga in this bitch. I plotted. I got something for her ass.

4 Saturday Night Live

Later that night, after I showered, I lounged on my big white couch in front of my fifty-two-inch TV wearing some black boy shorts and a baby tee. Hours had passed since we left the pool party yet, my phone was completely dry with the exception of Rodney sending multiple text messages asking me why I haven't responded to him all day. I texted Angela and filled her in on today's events, Camille FaceTime'd me but, still no word from Mike. I'm starting to think he's not going to hit me up because I went off on his chick. Then, I started to think if he's fucking with ratchet ass females like that Ashley bitch, I don't want him! THEN I remembered his tall sexy frame and his perfect ass teeth and instantly my pussy started to get wet. I hated that feeling of wanting something and not getting it. The last time I wanted something that I couldn't have was over two years ago when I attempted to purchase an expensive handbag online. The bag was in my shopping cart but right before I could checkout the website crashed. I was pissed. Frustrated for months. Now when it comes to a man that I've wanted and never gotten, well that's never actually happened.

Halfway through the movie, *Takers*, my intercom buzzes. I run over to it to answer.

"What's up, John?" John is the bellmen in the lobby of my apartment complex.

"Good evening, Ms. Roberts. You have a visitor."

"Who is it?" I anxiously asked.

"A Mr. Michael Keith."

Michael Keith? Wait, is that Mike? Oh shit! "Umm, you can send him up John."

I quickly ran to the bathroom to check my face. Slipped on some leggings over my boy shorts and put on some lip gloss. I didn't have time to put a bra on under my tee shirt before the doorbell rang. I was so fucking nervous! I gave myself one more glance over before I opened the door. There stood Mike, just like I expected, wearing True Religion dark denim belted by Damier print LV leather with a slim fit tee. His arms were so toned and his skin seemed to glow even in the dim hallway. In his hand he carried a bottle of red wine.

"You wanna come in?" I said as I slid to the side to let him walk in the door.

He still had that sexy ass smirk on his face as he greeted me and gave me hug. His arms were strong and he smelled so good, Polo Blue to be exact. He wrapped his arms around my waist.

"How'd you know where I stayed?" I asked as if I really cared.

"Yo homegirl gave me the info. My boy, Terry, hit her up and got the info for me. I woulda called, but I wanted to see the look on your face when I surprised you."

"Well, you definitely did. So, basically, I put my number in your phone for no reason," I flirtatiously snapped at him.

"Naw, not for no reason. I like that lil wink face you added though. Cute."

So he really did think about calling. I could not stop smiling.

"Well, I'm glad you came." It was the only thing I could think of to say at the moment.

"I know," he said confidently, which gave me goosebumps. His sex appeal is unbelievable.

Mike politely roamed around my apartment trying to get a feel for my personal style. He made no immediate remarks about anything but paused at a few family photos and art pieces that I have scattered around.

"You went to FAMU?" he asked while looking at my

undergrad degree that hung on the wall next to my office nook.

"I did. Most exciting four years of my life." He nodded in acceptance.

"Finance and business management." He read my degree.

"Where'd you go?" I was curious.

"I didn't. I barely made it out of high school," he admitted. I was shocked. He had to easily be making well over half a million in cash flow yearly just to afford the house I met him in earlier. To find out he didn't go to college was an eye opener.

"Don't try to treat me like a lame now." He leaned against my kitchen counter as I uncorked the wine.

I motioned him to hand me the wine glasses from the dish drainer. "Why would I do that?"

"A lot of females take that route when they find out I don't have a degree but then they see me pull out some cash or my black card and automatically assume I'm a dope boy."

"I could tell you weren't a dope boy."

"How?" He questioned, raising his eyebrows.

"Never met a dope boy that kept more than five

people in their house at a time and seeing that there had to be at least three hundred people at your house this afternoon, it's safe to say you have a different occupation," I clowned. He smiled.

He grabbed my hand and led me to the couch. He sat down and I sat down right next to him with my legs crossed over his. We sipped on the wine, watched the movie, and talked. I learned a lot about Michael Keith. He's a twenty-seven-year-old entrepreneur who owns a recording studio downtown. He was enthused about sharing his business aspirations and went into detail about his overall goals and objectives. I, in turn, went into depth about my career and he seemed really interested. By the time the movie credits were rolling, Mike and I were wrapped up in each other's arms making out. His lips were big and soft and he could not get enough of my lips. He gripped my ass with his hands and pulled me up on his lap. His lips moved from my lips to my neck and I instantly started to moan. He pulled my tee off and exposed my perky D breasts with both my nipples standing at attention. He put my left nipple in his mouth and started sucking while he grabbed my right tit with his free hand. My panties were soaking!

"Mike, stop." I blurted out even though I KNOW I didn't want him to stop.

He popped the titty out of his mouth and let go of my ass. He looked puzzled.

"What's wrong?" He asked in his very appealing voice.

"We can't do this, not now."

He seemed pissed at first then he seemed to look at ease.

"Alright," he said as he picked me up and placed me back on the couch.

"I didn't mean to make you uncomfortable Taya," he said sincerely as he helped me put my tee shirt back on.

"Trust me, I wasn't uncomfortable. I just can't have sex with you right now." I could tell by his facial expression that that answer was sufficient enough for him.

Mike stayed a little while longer and then I escorted him out the door. Later, as I lay in the bed, tonight's events just kept running through my mind. What the fuck was I thinking?! His sex appeal was all the way on and I'm sure he woulda fucked me good. But, I think I like Mike and I want him to respect me first, before I let him smash.

5 Random Visit

I was all the way gone last night. After it got dark and everybody was pretty much tired of swimming we brought the party inside. I had my boy, DJ Chance, on the second floor balcony filling the whole house with club bangers. We managed to run through two cases of Ciroc and a gallon of Henny. It got so wild that women started stripping, walking around and dancing nude. Like I said before, I always throw the best parties.

I woke up the next morning with my breath smelling like straight Hennessy. I went in my bathroom and found two naked chicks in my spa tub and a third chick laying on the floor. I stepped over shorty on the floor and proceeded to the sink to brush my teeth and wash the crust out my eyes. I slipped on some hoop shorts and walked out my room to see what the rest of the house was looking like.

I stood on the balcony overlooking my living room and all I could see was beer bottles covering the floor and a few puddles of vomit. Face down in one of those puddles was my boy Sly Hood. It was several motherfuckas passed out around the crib including Dre's ass. I went back in my room, grabbed my iPhone out my pants pocket, and called my usual cleaning crew to come a little earlier than scheduled.

After I rounded up all the hungover folks and put them out of my house; let the cleaning crew in, and got dressed, I headed to my office. I know it's Sunday, but a real businessman never stops working. Growing up I watched my mom hustle everyday of the week just to make sure me any my brother had fresh clothes to wear to school. So the only thing I knew, starting at a young age, was to grind to get mine.

"Good Morning, Mr. Keith." My secretary, Taylor, is always overly peppy.

"Can I get you anything sir?" She asked with this huge smile on her face, showing damn near all her teeth.

"Yea, I need some Advil, some Ray Bans, and all my messages from yesterday," I responded in the most unenthused tone.

"Long night, Mr. Keith?" She asked, still smiling.

"You have no idea," I commented as I stepped into my office.

A few minutes after I got settled at my desk and got my Mac running, Taylor came in with a cold glass of water and some Advil. She placed the shades on my eyes and handed me the pills, then motioned me to put them in my mouth and handed me the glass of water. This regiment had nearly become a weekly routine for her. She took out her iPhone and proceeded to read all my messages to me.

"There are forty-two messages, I'll start with the most urgent first and work my way down."

"Damn, forty-two? Over the weekend?"

"Yes, sir."

"Just give me the most urgent messages and delete the other ones."

"Yes, Mr. Keith. Message from Dorrian Phillips, Omni Theater Coordinator, called at 4:12pm confirming your venue booking for Next Month's Rap Battle." Taylor is articulate and talks extremely proper. "He states, and I quote, 'You may bring all your homies for VIP purposes.' Just be sure to send him the list ahead of time. Message from Cory Smith..." She rambles on.

As I sit and listen to Taylor talk her life away all I could think about was last night. Oh, I forgot to tell y'all what happened with Taya and I last night. It was nothing major, some light shit for real, but let me step back and give you the rundown.

So, Taya and Camille left the party pretty early.

Once they left, I went up to my boy, Terry, who had Camille in his face the whole time they were there. I asked him what info he had on them. He said that Taya was Sly's ex, which is funny because Sly and I just got real acquainted recently. He's headlining one of the beach parties I'm throwing this month, so it was nothing for me to hit him up and get the scoop on her. Terry mostly spoke about Camille and how he was sure he was going to get some action real soon. I pretended to pay attention but, I really was focused on the information he gave me about Sly and Taya. After I chopped it up with Terry I pulled out my phone and invited Sly over to the party. He initially declined my invite but, I was able to convince him to come after I described the layout of the party. Once he got to the crib, I got that fool stupid drunk and had him give me all the background info on Ms. Taya. It looked to me as if he was STILL sprung off that pussy, so I knew at that moment I had to try her and see what all the hype is about.

Sly drifted off into the past and recapped his first encounter with Taya. He also explained what it was like dating her. In the midst of rambling all her business off to me he told me which complex she stayed in Downtown. As ran his mouth I thought about making that move over to

Taya's crib. I mean things did kind of end abruptly with us and I didn't really want to take the typical "Hey what's up" text message approach. Once I got Sly to close his mouth I pawned him off on to one of my other homeboys and I made my final decision.

I hopped in my Benz, left my party, which was still fully cracking, and drove over to her complex. Let me clear some shit up, I ain't no stalking ass nigga, but I know I was on her mind and I knew for a fact she wanted to see a young nigga. Once I got to her complex I parked my shit and walked into the lobby. She lives in these tight ass penthouse apartments, high class for sure.

"Hello, sir. Can I help you?" The doorman asked.

"Yea, bro... Uhh, I'm here to see Taya," I responded quickly.

"Oh, Ms. Roberts? Is she expecting you?"

"Yea," I lied. I also wasn't sure if that was her last name but I took a chance.

"Ok, I'll buzz her for you," he said as he picked up the phone. "What's your name?"

"Michael Keith."

"Ms. Roberts, I have a Michael Keith here to see you... Yes... Michael Keith... Alright, I'll send him up." He hung up the phone. "She said you can go up, apartment 12F."

I was shocked. I wasn't expecting it to be that easy. I thought I was gon' have to get buck with buddy, but instead I'm getting on the elevator. By the time I got to the twelfth floor and got off, I was nervous as fuck. Anybody that knows me knows that's completely out of my character. I don't get nervous, especially not over a broad. I got to 12F and just stood there for a couple seconds. Checked my breath, made sure I was still looking fresh, and then I knocked on the door. *That wasn't no real nigga knock. Think she'll notice if I re-do my knock?*

In the midst of me trippin she opened the door. She was so bad! Man, I forgot how fine she was. Then I saw her again and I was ready to wife shorty. Her skin was so perfectly caramel with those long ass eyelashes, and her lips just a perfect shade of pink. Not to mention how fat her ass is! She had on some black leggings and all her ass was sticking out and then on top of that she had on a white midriff with no bra. Man...

"What are you doing here?" The first thing she said with a slight attitude.

"To see you," I said, suave as hell despite my

nervousness.

"Right, but how did you find out where I live?"

"Yo friend," I stated vaguely. I neglected to mention Sly.

"You want to come in?" She said as she stepped to the side to let me in.

I walked in and she closed the door behind us. And then I grabbed her by the waist and she embraced me trying to hold back her smile.

"I definitely didn't know you were coming over here," she said with this big ass smile on her face.

"I like surprising people." I said releasing her from our embrace.

"Well, I'm glad you came."

"I know," I said confidently.

I could tell she was feeling the whole Money Mike swag. Most chick's fuck with it, some think I'm too cocky and others think it's sexy as fuck.

We sat on the couch in Taya's clean ass all white living room. Sipping red wine, watching *Takers*. The movie was playing, but we spent most of the time talking to each other. She was really interested in my career and what I like to do in my free time.

"I'm the Founder and CEO of Shutdown Studio, downtown Miami," I explained.

"That's like five minutes from here. I've seen that place a thousand times. So, you work a lot?"

"I don't think of it as working. It's more like a lifestyle. I love my company and all its components so, naturally, I spend a lot of my time making it better. What do you do?"

"Well, I'm a Senior Marketing VP for Alcore Software. I used to do a lot of designing for campaigns and front line marketing, but now I manage a pretty large group on how to perform some of those same skill sets."

"I see you out here grindin just like me."

"Probably a little bit harder." She joked.

"So let me ask you something?" she changed the subject,

"What you got?"

"That chick from earlier, the one that was all up in my face. What's her deal?"

I rolled my eyes. "Man, to be honest, she not shit. That was one of my jump offs that got way too attached."

Her expression showed some resistance to my answer. Now that I think about it, I probably shouldn't have described Ashley that way. But it was the truth.

"What do you do in your free time?" I changed the subject immediately.

She took a sip from her glass and then answered. "I shop and party pretty much," she laughed.

"That's funny because that's what I do for a living and that's what you do for fun," I responded.

"I know. I see you throw pretty big parties. Are all your parties like that?"

"Naw, they're usually a lot bigger."

"Damn, really?"

"For real, I pretty much know everybody in the city."

She looked intrigued and worried at the same time. I could tell what she was thinking about: how many hoes has this dude slept with, is he like the typical trifling dudes that I'm used to dealing with, and do I want to go through some bullshit with this guy. So, before she could start asking me those questions, I kissed her. She fell into my arms and let me grab whatever I wanted. She had these super soft ass lips that I couldn't help but suck on. I palmed her ass and pulled her up on my lap, then I lifted up her shirt all while our lips were still interlaced. I put her tit in my mouth and went to work. Her skin was soft and moisturized. My hands roamed freely across her body, exploring every inch. I was plotting on how I was gon get those leggings off when she stopped me.

"Mike, stop," she said like it was urgent.

I just looked at her.

"We can't do this," she stated.

Yes, the fuck we can. I thought. But instead of responding that way, I sat her back on the couch and helped her put her shirt back on.

Man, she had my dick all the way hard. Every sexual position that I could think of rushed my mind as my hands remembered the softness of her skin. I played it cool. I was comfortable with her decision. One thing that I could always count on is a female's ability to be indecisive. They never know what they want. We finished watching the movie and continued our conversation like nothing ever happened. When I said my goodbyes, I told her I would hit her up and headed back to my party.

*****

Taylor was still rambling off all my messages.

"Taylor..."

"Yes, Mr. Keith?" she said, still smiling.

"Thought you were only going to read me the urgent messages."

"These are all the urgent messages, there's only a few more left. Would you like me to finish?"

"Hell no. Just delete em. I'll let you know if I need anything."

Taylor left my office, closing the door behind her. I sat at my desk replaying the events of last night. I knew I had a little more work to do in order to take Taya for that test drive. I was up for the challenge.

6 A little Thunder

Life can be funny sometimes, one day you're fucking your co-worker's boyfriend and the next you're tryna stop yourself from fucking a perfectly available man.

I was up making breakfast in my tee shirt and panties ... well, no tee shirt, just panties, jamming to some Neo Soul. My weekend has been pretty live thus far but I'm ready to wind down. I have so much to do for this upcoming work week but I can't seem to get Mike off my mind. *Should I just call him or should I wait for him to call me?* Just as I was having that debate with myself, my phone rang. I anxiously pick up my phone just to be disappointed by the sight of Rodney's name on my screen. I politely reject the call and go back to cooking my breakfast.

While I ate my scrambled egg whites and toast, I thought about Mike, more specifically, the sex I wanted to have with him. I'm quite adventurous in between the sheets, but it seems like Mike is more of the aggressor and I would get off more if I was completely submissive, allowing him to do what he chose to with my thick ass. I imagined the impact of his strong hands as he pulled himself deeper inside as his lips lightly pressed against my neck while he stroked.

After breakfast, I sat in my home office and got some work done. A few hours passed and I became bored. So, of course, I called Camille.

"What's up, Taya?"

"Let's do something."

"Shit, I'm down. What you wanna do? Club? Lounge? Party?"

"I honestly just wanna do something chill, like dinner and drinks."

"You know what, there's that new restaurant that opened up downtown. Heard all the ballers been in there lately!"

"Sounds like the move. I'll pick you up in an hour," I offered.

"Cool, I'ma tell Angela and Danielle to meet us there," she suggested.

"Alright." I hung up the phone and went directly into my walk-in closet. When I came out I was fully fitted in some black fitted jeans, black sheer button down blouse with a red push up bra, and red Louboutin pumps accompanied by my large LV Damier handbag. Fresh, of course.

I hopped in my Beamer, dropped the top, and headed to Camille's crib. She lives about twenty minutes from where I stay, which is a tad bit out of the way seeing that we were going to a spot on my side of town. But, I don't like to go to the club in separate cars, especially if I plan on drinking.

We pulled up to The Blue Room downtown. I allowed valet to take my car and we headed for the door. As we were walking in we noticed some of the Oklahoma City Thunder players standing outside. They just played against the Miami Heat earlier today and were still in town.

"You weren't lying! All the ballers are in this joint. Literally!"

"Hell yea! Glad I put on this bombshell bra," Camille commented.

We busted out laughing as we entered in the building. We spotted Angela and Danielle at the bar.

"What's good!!" Camille anxiously exclaimed as we took a seat next to them.

"Hey, Tay, hey, Cam," Danielle greeted us as Angela waved while she sipped her drink.

Danielle was one of our homegirls from college. She just moved back to Miami after living overseas for the last two years with her European boyfriend. Clearly things didn't work out.

"So, Danielle what happened with you and Jahn-Paul? I was sure y'all was about to get married the way he swept you off your feet," Camille asked.

"Girl, it was all good for a while. We were vibing and living up that Euro lifestyle. But shit got crazy a couple months ago," Danielle began.

"Crazy like baby mama crazy?" Angela asked.

"No, girl, worse. Look, so about two months ago I started noticing Jahn was getting off work extra late regularly. He claimed his company picked up a new demanding client that requested he worked late."

"So was he lying?" I asked.

"Naw he wasn't lying. His client did request additional time from him but it wasn't work related," she continued. We all gasped.

"Long story short. One day I go to our apartment during lunch because I forgot my wallet and needed to grab it really quick. Why did I come home to Jahn-Paul in the bed—"

"Fucking another bitch," Camille interrupted.

"No, he was fucking another man!"

"Aw hell naw!!" We all yelled at the same time.

"So needless to say, I packed all my shit up that night and got the fuck out. It took me a couple weeks to get all my stuff and myself out of there but I had to go. And don't think I didn't take some of his money and jewelry with me on the way out the door."

"I feel you on that one," Camille said. "These men out here are so shady. Not only do we have to worry about bitches throwing themselves at our men but now we gotta worry about other men!"

"Hell naw, I woulda had to catch a case," Angela proclaimed.

"Exactly, I'm not about to play around with these confused men. It's either you like women or you like men but, you aint getting both with me. Anyway, I got ghost on his ass. But enough about that asshole. What new men y'all got creepin in y'all lives," the nosey gossip girl came out.

"Taya the only one that gets play around here," Camille snitched and I gave her the side eye.

"Ok, Ms. Taya. Who you got up next?" Danielle probed.

"Well... I am kind of interested in this guy I met this weekend. Fine ass successful cocoa brown man," I vividly described.

"Is he well known? I know you and you don't become interested in everyday regular men. Who is he?" She kept probing.

"Yea, I guess you can say he's well known." I rolled my eyes. "His name is Money Mike."

"Money Mike that owns Shutdown Studios? The Mike that throws all the hottest A list parties?" she asked.

"Yea, that's him." Camille added.

"Well damn, you go girl." She expressed her consent then raised her hand prompting me for a high five. I accepted even though I thought she was being extra.

"So anyway, what's the scene looking like in here?" I said.

"It's nothing but super fine ass athletes and rappers, and a sprinkle of successful good looking suit wearing brothers!" Angela excitedly described to us.

"Just how I like it," I said as I flipped my hair. The bartender asked me for my drink order. "Let me get a Red Berry Ciroc and Red Bull please." Just as I finished my order, a tall figure interrupts.

"You can put that on my tab" a smooth deep voice said.

I turned around in my seat, and let my eyes roll all the way up this tall figure. It was none other than six-feet ten inch Kenneth Clemson standing in front of me. I just sat there completely speechless. My nosey girls chattered in the background.

"What's up," he asked as he took a seat next to me.

I had to get myself together. Get back on my swag. I turned around on the bar stool so that I was facing him with my back to my girls.

"You tell me what's up." These were the only words I could even think of but I said it in my "completely flirtatious Taya way".

"I just find it hard to let gorgeous women pay for their own drinks," he said as he scanned my silhouette.

I've met plenty of basketball players before, so I already know what they want. They just want something fine to fuck for the night. And while I like to think that I have morals and standards, KC had my pussy all the way wet off the strength that he was damn near seven feet alone.

The bartender brought my drink and Ken laid a fifty dollar bill down and told her to keep the change.

I smiled and extended my hand. "I greatly appreciate it. My name is Taya."

He grabbed my hand. "Do I need to introduce myself?"

Of course he didn't! "Nah, I'm familiar," I responded.

We exchanged comments, flirted, and mingled. He was intriguing and knew how to hold a conversation. His personality plus the fact that he was a well known all star NBA player sparked my interest. Highly desired men were always naturally appealing to me. I found gratification from attracting men that were commonly labeled as "off the market" or "hard to get to". Plus, KC was attractive. After I finished my drink, I handed the valet ticket for my car to Camille and left with KC.

Before I knew it, I was in a King size hotel bed with Ken's dick sliding in and out of me. His dick was just like him, long and slim. His stroke game was all the way on point; I could tell he gets pussy all the time. He palmed both my tits in his hands like he would a basketball and pushed my legs up by my head while he fucked the shit outta me. I couldn't even contain my moans, he had my juices flowing! He flipped me over, buried my face in a pillow, pulled my hands around my back, and beat it up doggy style. All you could hear was my ass smacking up against his abs and my muffled moans under the pillow. Ten minutes later he filled the condom up with cum and was laid out on the bed as if he had just finished an intense basketball game.

The first thing that came out of his mouth was, "Damn that pussy was right!"

I laughed. We laid naked in his bed staring out of the Victorian windows at the busy city that was thriving while we chilled. He was so funny and entertaining. I fell in love with his company. After a while, the wine bottle was getting low and the time was passing us by so I told Ken I needed to start getting ready to head back to my place.

"Taya, make sure your number is saved in my phone before you leave."

That was a first. Basketball players normally don't remember names and they damn sure don't care about your phone number. "Alright. I got you." I picked up his iPhone, put my number in there, and saved under my name with a wink emoji behind it.

After we showered together and got fresh he walked me down to the limo, kissed me my forehead, and told me he would hit me up eventually. The limo took me to Camille's house where I picked up my BMW. Camille wouldn't let me walk out the door without telling her every detail of my night. She told me she knew I was going to pull a hooper. She claimed she felt it coming. Her theory was that though I seemed to be really interested in Money Mike I was more invested in my own personal brand. The Taya Roberts brand that depicted me as a trophy to be won in some sort of hypothetical competition. To sum up her theory, she thought I was more intrigued by the thrill of being courted rather than an actual relationship. I simply told her her theory was wrong; I just haven't known Mike long enough to take him seriously yet. We agreed to disagree. Then, I grabbed my keys and headed back to my side of town.

7 Typical Monday

My least favorite day of the week is Monday. Not because it's the day after the weekend or because of my hangovers from the night before. It's because every single Monday my schedule is jammed packed with people who swear this is their week to get it together. Those same people who bullshit Tuesday through Friday and use Monday as a catch up day.

This morning at six a.m. I had an update meeting that was marked as urgent with some partners whose office is located on the east coast. When I got on the phone with the operational staff at a regular night club I work with they had a list of new regulations they wanted to share with me. Shit like "Starting this weekend we cannot allow guest to pour liquor on females" or "we aren't allowing smoking in the private sections anymore."

I always sit there quietly, barely listening until I hear a pause for my turn to speak. Then I politely tell they ass, "I have no control over what people do once they are in your establishment. But what I do have control of are the five hundred plus VIP tickets I sell each weekend." And then I remind them that if those sales are seeming to hurt their business then I can contract elsewhere. Then I pause and listen to them attempt to retract all their previous statements. I honestly couldn't care less about them sending apologies, I just need my monthly cut off the door. That's it. These repetitive meetings continued all morning and I continued to put people in their place.

This particular morning, I had an unusual visitor walk into my office. My fine ass ex Danielle. I dated her for two years then she left me for some French motherfucka and moved away. And now she was standing in my lobby waiting to talk to me.

"Mr. Keith..." Taylor greeted as she poked her head in my door.

"Come in, Taylor." Taylor walked in looking annoyed which is completely out of her character.

"What's up?"

"So Danielle is still in the lobby. And she's getting a tad bit bold with me."

"Did she tell you what she wanted?"

"She wouldn't tell me. She said, and I quote..." Taylor looked down at her notepad and began reading, "...it's none of my effing business."

"I'll handle it. Send her in." Taylor stepped out and

a few moments later Danielle walked in.

I didn't even stand up to greet her. I just watched her walk in and take a seat at my desk. I met Danielle in a night club. She was the "stuck up, too good to be in the club" type. Just like I like. I spit some game on her one time and had her going for me that night. She was cool, chill, and fine. After over a year of hitting literally whenever I wanted, I gave her a promotion and cuffed her. She was high maintenance, snobby and nosey. But, she was super submissive in the bedroom and treated me like a king. Except for those days when she thought I was cheating, then she tried to handle me like a bitch. She got tired of my lifestyle; the late nights, the bitches and the parties. And I got tired of her mouth.

"Hello, Michael," she said with this little devious smirk.

"Danielle Stewart," I mocked. "Who do I owe for this visit?"

"I just simply thought I'd stop by and see how an old friend was doing. I see you still fine as ever."

"Yea and I see you still running that same ass played game you always ran. You looking good too." I didn't lie. She was looking fine. You can tell she been getting that cardio work in the gym and them titties were sitting perfect. Not to mention her pretty ass eyes.

She laughed. "Played game? Who me?" She mocked me back. "Look. Let's have dinner tonight. My treat. I wanna do some catching up."

"I don't know about that," I answered, shaking my head.

"Really, Mike? Just dinner. How harmless is that?" She asked, touching my hand. I forgot how charming she can be. She's literally the female version of myself when it comes to running game.

"Fine. Just a quick dinner and that's it."

"Cool," she said, smiling as she stood up. "I'll speak with your little secretary and have her add me to your schedule."

I sat there in awe as she left. Not from her presence but, from the fact that she came back. I was certain she was gone for good. She was always the type to stand by her decisions. I can't believe I let this woman swindle her way into my life once again. I'm pretty sure dude she was with played her and now she's running back to a real man. But, honestly, I'm pretty sure I wasn't bouta give her no play. I was curious. Just wanted to see where I stood.

Taylor waked in. "Mr. Keith, you have another visitor."

My day continued like this all the way until I was ready to go home.

8 Did That Ass a Favor

I woke up, thanks to my alarm, promptly at 6:30am. I was completely worn the fuck out from last night. Ciroc and Red Bull plus KC's long ass left me completely drained. But, nonetheless, I was up and focused on a successful day. I showered in my large walk-in shower with the water almost near scorching. I hopped out smelling like lavender thanks to my shower gel. I put on a small amount of makeup and flat ironed my hair. By the time I was ready to walk out the door, I was fully suited; looking real fresh and professional.

I arrived to work at 8:30, the main receptionist, Kate, greeted me. "Good morning, Ms. Roberts," she smiled.

"Morning," I said casually as I approached the elevator.

I stood in front of the elevator sipping my morning hot chocolate. Keith from accounting walked up and waited with me.

"Good Morning, Taya. How was your weekend?"

"It was ok," I said like I didn't just get through washing KC's scent off my body last night or almost beat a bitch's ass on Saturday.

The elevator finally came and just my luck none other than Ty, Rodney's girlfriend, was already on. I could tell she knew something because the look this girl gave me would have killed me, if it were possible.

"What's up, Ty?" I asked, even though I really didn't care.

"Hey... Taya," she forced out of her mouth.

The elevator stopped on my floor and I got off. If she has beef with me she'll address it, until then I really couldn't care less.

I entered my office and started my day. Mondays are always busy. My schedule was packed with relevant and irrelevant meetings plus I had to complete a major promotion storyline for some executives. I always liked to start the week off with a staff meeting in my office. This is where all the junior directors brought in their production metrics from the previous week and attempted to shit on one another. I enjoyed the competition between my directs. The art of competition motivates individuals to do their best every day, which works out for me perfectly because every last one of them were exceeding the company's expectations. If they're successful, I'm successful. It's really that simple.

By the time lunch came around I was exhausted and starving. I normally don't take a lunch break but from the lack of a well-balanced breakfast this morning I needed a meal.

"Hold all my calls for the next hour, I'm going to lunch," I buzzed my secretary, Jane. Jane's my fourth secretary this year. Most of my admins quit once they see how late I stay some nights and I require them to stay until I leave. But Jane has been holding up pretty good so far plus, she enjoys the overtime. She's at least ten years older than me, single, with no kids. She is a perfectionist which makes her nearly perfect as an administrative assistant.

I grabbed my purse and headed for my Range Rover. On my way to the car, I peeped Ty mugging me again! I knew something was about to go down soon. When I got to the car I checked my cell phone. Four missed calls and two text messages from Rodney. I finally called him back. I was sick of him blowing up my phone. I know the pussy was good, but damn, it couldn't have been that good.

"Hello?" He answered.

"What's the deal, Rodney?" I said with a slight attitude.

"Why you been ignoring my calls?" he squealed! His impatient eagerness for me to simply tell him why I haven't been answering his calls were simply unattractive. And to think I thought this man was fine just a few days ago.

"Boy, it ain't like you're my dude! I don't have to answer your calls. You were a lil booty call that wasn't worth shit!"

"Bitch please. You were all on my dick, thirsty as hell!"

"Yea until I realized you was a quick pumper!"

"It ain't my fault yo pussy was extra tight and wet! You caught a nigga off guard, plus I was drunk!"

I busted out laughing. We were both drunk but that still doesn't excuse his lackadaisical penis. If anything, being drunk should make you last longer.

"Well anyway, why you been blowing me up?" I continued our conversation.

"I been tryna tell you that Ty saw yo name in my phone and been questioning me bout that shit. I told her it was a different Taya. I was tryna give you the heads up," he explained.

"Oh, damn. That's why she been mugging. Alright, cool. Don't worry. I'll handle it."

"Alright, bet. So, when we fucking again?"

I hung up the phone in his face. I wasn't even about to give him the chance to open up that conversation again. But, I'm glad we cleared that up, I'll handle Ty's ass a little bit later. I knew something was up but, now it's clear she knows.

I checked my two unread texts. One was from KC:

Ken 8:49am
Good Morning Sexy

I laughed out loud. I wasn't expecting that from him, but I must admit I was loving the attention. I texted back:

Me 12:03pm
Gm. You must miss me already?

I checked my second text:

Mike 9:45am
What's good?

That's all he has to say to me after not hitting me up for damn near two days! I didn't even text him back I was so pissed. What pissed me off the most was the fact that he has been occupying my mind non-stop over the weekend but clearly it's not that deep for him. I thought men liked women who didn't give up the ass on the first night but, I could be wrong about that as well. I drove to my favorite deli, sat down, ate lunch, and then headed back to work.

When I got to my desk I buzzed Jane. "Jane can you contact Tyesha Alexander and tell her to meet me in my office ASAP." It was time to nip this shit.

About thirty minutes passed before Ty knocked on my glass door. I took her tardiness as blatant disrespect. I motioned for her to come in. She closed the door behind her.

"Have a seat," I told her as I directed her with my hand.

Ty's cute. She's not extremely impressive nor is she hideous. She's your simple average every day cute chick. A nice face, an average length hair weave, and a basic wardrobe. Plain but cute.

"Ms. Roberts how can I help you," she spoke but I could hear her attitude.

I got up and walked over to my door to let down the privacy shade then I paced around the room as I spoke.

"I'm going to skip the bullshit," I said in a calm, soft voice.

She looked at me with piercing eyes.

"I know how hard you've been working on our new printer campaign and I can admit that you've been doing a pretty average job," I politely insulted her. "I'd hate for all your hard work to go to waste just because you can't seem to control your attitude every time I'm in your presence," I threatened as I took the seat right next to her. "So let's address your problem before you cost yourself your job," I smiled.

"Where was Rodney on Friday night?" she demanded.

"Rodney?" I played dumb just for the sake of personal entertainment.

"Yes Rodney. My boyfriend," she snapped.

"Why are you asking me? Shouldn't you know? Isn't that your man?" I added pessimistically.

"It's just funny how I introduced y'all that afternoon then, later on, he doesn't come home and the next day your name is in his phone," she rolled her neck.

"I think it's funny that in less than eight hours I was able to get your man to not go home. I must say I am impressed," I complimented myself.

She stood up. I stood up too.

"Truth is you got a "pass around" for a boyfriend. One of those niggas that is for everybody. If it weren't me, it would have been somebody else. But luckily for you I don't want his ass."

"You, bitch," she scowled.

"Watch your tone and your language. Remember I'm your boss's boss. So, if I want you gone then you'll be non-existent to this marketing team. So is there anything else you'd like to say?" I folded my arms.

"Stay away from my man."

"Again, I do not want him. Do me a favor and tell him to stop calling me." She rolled her eyes.

"Now if there isn't anything else, get out of my office." She stormed out and slammed the door behind her and I continued on with my day like nothing happened.

I went the rest of my workday without seeing Ty again, what a coincidence. I could care less though. Rodney will just have to deal with her. I wasn't concerned with their relationship and quite frankly I'm a bit sour that I had to spend a portion of my day reminding the both of them of that. After a few more meetings I packed up my briefcase and headed out the door.

"Have a wonderful evening, Ms. Roberts," Kate stated as I walked out of the main entrance.

On my way home I copped a bottle of white wine, pasta, and chicken. I'm making chicken parmesan for dinner. On my way out of the grocery store my phone started ringing. Despite my fumbling threw my purse to find my smart phone I still managed to answer before they hung up. It was Mike.

"Hello?" I answered.

"What's good?" *Here he goes with that "what's good" bullshit.*

"Nothin is good, Mike! Why haven't I heard from you?"

"What you mean, girl? It's only been like two days."

"I just assumed after the night we spent together you woulda hit me up!"

"Well, I would assume the same from you," he said in his smooth, calm tone.

I was stuck. He was right. I could've hit his phone just as much as he could've hit mine. In fact, he texted me this morning and I let my stubbornness take over and didn't text him back.

"You're right," I admitted.

"I know," he said confidently. "You should come over tonight."

At the moment I couldn't stand him, but his offer was very tempting. I had a long eventful day and I wouldn't mind some company from the opposite sex. His cocky and smooth demeanor definitely helped persuade my decision.

"I'll be over in an hour," I told him.

"Hurry up," he demanded.

I went home, put the wine on chill, and got in the shower. *What am I going to wear?* Of course, I'm gonna be sexy, but how sexy? I got out of the shower and put on some black panties with a matching push up halter bra. I pulled a short, tight red halter dress over my body and, of course, it fit like a glove. I looked good. My hair was straight down my back and the black pumps that I put on made my legs look amazing.

I pulled into Mike's driveway an hour and a half after we got off the phone, walked up to the door with the wine and knocked. My adrenaline was pumping. He opened the door seconds later. Damn he was fine. His chocolate complexion makes me melt. He stood in the doorway with his polo tee shirt and Levi jeans on like he didn't even try to look good. He grabbed my hand and pulled me in the house, took the bottle from my hand, and embraced me. "You look good as fuck."

I smiled. "Thank you."

His house is huge. You can tell it had been

professionally decorated and it is impeccably clean. The first level is open and inviting. The living room was covered wall to wall in marble floor and decorated with classy leather furniture with a large fireplace as the focal point. The kitchen is off to the right. Near the front door is a breakfast nook that was adjacent to a very long and narrow kitchen that led to the dining room in the back. It appeared to be no bedrooms on the first level. Overlooking the living room is a large indoor balcony. The stairwell to the second level is hidden in the furthermost left hand corner of the living space. There were no pictures of him, or any other people for that matter, just a few splashes of art tastefully placed in various places around the home.

After giving me a tour of his house, Mike grilled chicken and asparagus for dinner on his fully furnished patio. We socialized over cocktails while he finished grilling and I enjoyed the nice late night Florida breeze. While we ate in the dining room we had an interesting discussion about each of our days at work. Turns out Mike had a similar hectic day at his office. I neglected to mention my little conversation with Ty. I didn't think he needed to know those types of details. After dinner we migrated to the living room and made ourselves comfortable on the couch.

"We should go ahead and set up our next date so you won't trip on me for not calling," Mike said, smiling.

"Oh so you're saying you wanna see me again," I flirtatiously added.

"Of course. It's only a matter of time before I start calling you mine."

"Why are you so sure?" I was curious.

He laughed. "I usually get any and everything I want." He slid his hand around my waist and pulled me closer. "And I want you," he boldly said while looking me dead in my face.

"Well, you're going to have to show me that you deserve somebody like me."

"Bet," he said confidently, like he already knew he won me over.

"So you remember when you and your lil friend crashed my party?"

"Yea," I said, laughing.

"Well, I remember that you can dance pretty good. I want a personal dance."

"A personal dance?"

"Yea girl. You smart, you know what personal and dance mean. Matter fact, how bout you strip for me. I got some twenties in my pocket."

I laughed but he was looking so serious. And I personally love a challenge. "Where's the music?" I asked as I stood up.

Mike turned on his surround sound, dimmed the lights, and got real comfortable. I danced for him, sexy and seductive. I unzipped my dress and let it slide off my body. My ass was thick as hell in my black lace thong and my twins sat upright in my halter push up bra. Every female knows that if there is even a slight chance that you may get some action you must make sure the bra and panty set are on point. Mike looked pleased and I could see his dick start to poke out in his jeans.

"Damn, baby! Come here," he said with his arms open.

I slid in his arms and he immediately palmed my ass. I gave him a lap dance. By the time the next song ended I could tell he was ready to fuck.

"Let's go in the room," he said anxiously.

Before I even answer he picked me up and carried me to his bedroom. We passionately embraced each other with our lips as he carried me up the marble staircase and down the hall to his room. Mike threw me on the bed and took his shirt off. His abs and arms are amazingly cut up. He pulled his jeans off and stood there in his boxers. Then, he pulled his boxers off. The sight of his dick made my pussy drip. He climbed on the bed and slid between my legs.

"I been thinking bout getting inside of you for the last two days."

He took my bra off exposing my supple D breasts with my nipples inviting him to suck them. And that's exactly what he did. I moaned. That shit felt amazing. I grabbed the back of his head trying to control myself. After he played with my nipples with his tongue he came up for air. With my hands around his neck he grabbed my waist and flipped me over on top of him. He put his hands behind his head and relaxed against the pillows with a slick smile on his face. I slid down his body until his penis was in my face and then I shoved it to the back of my throat.

"Oh shit!" were the only words he could get out of his mouth.

I locked my jaws around his dick and slurped it like I would a Popsicle. I could feel his blood rushing and his balls tighten up. So, I stopped. I'm trying to feel him inside of me and if I make him cum that would postpone the fucking. Mike pulled me back up to his face and pulled my panties off, all in one motion. Then he pushed his raw dick inside my soaking wet lips. I immediately started bouncing on his dick. I pressed my hands up against his strong chest to get a better grip and I fucked his dick until I couldn't take it anymore. He pulled me off of him and threw me on an empty space on the bed. He stood up with his wet manhood sticking out. He slid me to the end of the bed and put it back it in.

"I just wanna fuck you forever but this shit way too tight to last forever," he said as he palmed my breasts.

He made sure he was ALL the way inside every time he thrust in and out. My moans were outta control at this point and I knew I was about to climax at any moment. He started fucking me harder and faster! I gripped the sheets as I let off a loud moan and covered his penis in a silky white cream. Even though I came Mike was still going strong. He flipped me over so that my ass was sticking out in the air and he went back in. I arched my back and spread my legs. He gripped my ass as he super stroked all my wetness. The sound of my ass smacking up against him must have turned him on because he undoubtedly beat my shit up! He pulled out and busted all over my back. Whew!

"Get up," he said while slapping me on my ass.

I got up a followed him to the bathroom. He turned on the shower and then walked over to me, put his hands around my waist, and started passionately kissing me. He seemed like he genuinely was enjoying my company. I was speechless. I was spending the evening with a highly successful, fine ass man who cooked me dinner and piped me down something serious. There was nothing to say. I got in the shower first, then Mike got in and closed the door. We both rinsed the sticky residue of sex of our bodies. There were two shower heads so we both could bathe individually, but Mike was still all over me. Grabbing and kissing and sucking all over my body.

"Damn, did you not got enough of me yet?" I asked him while he had my ass in both of his hands and one of my nipples in his mouth.

"You so fucking bad naked. I just can't keep my hands off of you," he said then he went back to sucking my tit. I was definitely feeling myself after that comment. We bathed ourselves, then each other. And then Mike ended up fucking me against the shower glass. He held me up by my thighs and maneuvered in and out by controlling his waist. When he had enough he pulled out and let his passion go into the shower stream. After we showered,

Mike dried me off, rubbed lotion over my body and carried me to his bed. I passed out in his king sized bed with his arms wrapped around me.

I woke up a few hours later and snuck downstairs to find my clothes. I slipped on my dress and walked out the door. I wanted to spend the night but I had to get up in a few hours to get ready for work. Mike will understand. That man was knocked the fuck out anyway, he'll never even know I left.

9 Chopped It Up with My boys

I don't give a fuck about too much other than my girl and my money. And today a bitch nigga was tryna fuck with both of them.

"Money Mike, bro, no offense to you but Taya…oh weee…" Dom, this shady ass dude I do business with, decided to comment on Taya. He paused and collected his thoughts. "She bad as fuck."

"Tell me something I don't know," I said, folding my arms and rearing back at my desk.

"I saw her the other night at Jasmine's. She was wearing this little red dress. Man… I'll pay you to let me just taste that."

"Dog. You need to pay me for this event you want me to host. And keep my girl out yo thoughts." This motherfucka lost his mind. Dom's face went from an eager overly playful smile to a smug serious look.

"So before I cut this check, I just need to make sure we on the same page as far as how many guests your business plans on bringing in." Dom went back to discussing business.

"Man do you know who you talking to? I'll bring in as many guests as I want to. I'll have the whole city show up if that check fat enough. Just show me the commas and I'll get it cracking." *I can't believe he trying me like this.*

"I know you the man, Money Mike. I'm just tryna make sure we clear," he said as he pulled out his checkbook. "If I throw an extra grand in can you get Taya to show up?" he laughed.

"As long as you put another couple G's away for your hospital bill cause you gone need that shit if you bring her name up again." I was serious.

"I'm joking, bro" he laughed then handed me the check.

I reviewed the amount then I signed our contract and handed him his copy. After Dom's hoe ass got the fuck out my office I called Taylor in.

"Yes, Mr. Keith."

"Deposit this check for me." I handed her the check.

"Got it."

"What else is on my schedule today?"

She pulled out her iPad. "You have lunch and then you're scheduled to play basketball with Dre."

"Cool." I was relieved to have a break this afternoon

after the morning I've been having. An afternoon chilling with my boys would be better than sitting on these conference calls.

If I used the term "best friend" I would say Dre is the equivalent to that. He and I been down with each other since grade school. Dre's the type of dude that you can rely on if some shit goes down but he also that same nigga that probably got you in that situation to begin with. He always been the type to talk first then think after the fact, which gets him into a lot of uncalled for trouble.

If Dre didn't work for me he would be in the streets with the dope boys. I gave him the position of Events Manager just to keep his ass away from the streets. He manages all my club relationships with the promoters and owners. He's never in the office because he's literally always on the go. But he loves that shit. That was the only thing that kept him from getting a nine to five was the fact that he would have to be in an office all day like me. As long as all my events and parties happen on time and as scheduled I couldn't give a fuck if he worked out the strip club, which he does from time to time.

Later that day, I hooped it up with my boys. We got in a few solid games of three on three full court. Me, Dre, and Rashad on one team, Terry, Lo, and Sosa on the other. Dre and I use to hoop together in high school and been playing street ball together since like the fourth grade. We picked up Rashad a few years back once we saw him give these niggas the post game work at a Florida State home game. Terry, Lo, and Sosa some typical hooping niggas. They're good competition but they can't touch us.

"Damn we dubbed y'all again," Dre bragged.

"Man y'all still ain't shit. Run that shit back," Terry bitched.

"Naw, man. I need to get back to the office. Handle some grown man business," I told him.

"Yea me too. Shit been getting hella crazy on my internship. I wasn't even gone be able to get off but Money Mike dropped a word on my boss," Rashad told everyone as he expressed his gratitude by dapping me up.

"It ain't shit bro," I assured him.

Rashad graduated from Florida State a few months back and was having a hard time finding a job despite the fact that he had a Bachelor's Degree in Business Management. I called up a few of my boys that run their own business or hold a VP position at top corporate firms and used a few of my favors. Before Rashad knew it, he had more offers on the table than he could even deal with. He swung by my office one day and we hashed out all the details. Thought through which position suited him more, cultures that he thought he would fit into, and most importantly who was offering the most money. After a few sessions, he took a paid internship with 3M as a Business Analyst. My dude doing pretty good for himself now.

"So, Mike, let me ask you something?" I could tell Terry was about to be nosey.

"What bro?"

"How you managing Ms. Taya? Word on the street is you cuffed that," he pried.

"Oh, that's the word?" I entertained the conversation.

"I mean, I'm just tryna figure it. I'm just curious.".

"So this what you can tell the streets and anybody that ask: Taya, that's me." Then I took a sip from my water bottle.

In unison, everybody seemed shocked and gasping for air. They just had to be all dramatic and shit.

"Wow, bro. Never thought I'd see the day Money Mike started claiming somebody," Terry said.

"Shit when you find something you like might as

well put yo stamp on her. Cause you know how these niggas are. Always plotting on the next bitch." Dre dapped me up.

"Man I'm tryna find me a shorty like that. Something just as bad as Taya and on her own shit," Terry added. Things with Terry and Camille must have not been going as he expected judging by the way he spoke.

"Why haven't I heard of this woman?" Rashad asked, unlacing his sneakers.

"Naw you've seen her before, trust me. Especially if you were at Mike's pool party; she was that bad ass chick wearing that thin ass pink bikini," Terry explained, laughing.

I didn't laugh. I just observed these niggas critiquing my chick. The shit was actually entertaining. To these dudes Taya was like some untouchable supermodel that you could only look at and they were idolizing me for dating her.

"So anyway, what y'all got up tonight?" Dre always tryna figure out the next move.

Everybody immediately looked over to me. "Yea, Mike, what we getting into?" Terry questioned.

"It's whatever, man. Solo's having a social event. Probably be a lot of fine women in there I'm sure," I added. Solo's is a night lounge on the south end of downtown.

"I'm down," Rashad stated.

"Consider the shit handled. I'll have y'all added to my VIP list," I confirmed.

"Once again, Money Mike comes through in the clutch. 'Preciate it, bro," Terry said.

"Don't even mention it. I'm out though. I'll see y'all later." I made my exit.

It's always cool catching up with my boys. They remind me why I have to keep grinding. It's either get out here and make more money or end up working a dead end nine to five. The choice is mine.

10 Summer Jam

I never miss my money, regardless of the encounters I had the night before. I couldn't give two fucks if it was raining, sleeting, or if I fucked a ten-inch penis in the shower. I will have my ass at work. One thing my parents taught me was a strong work ethic. I'm a high maintenance, halfway bougie female that can't seem to go five days without a fresh pedicure. With a mentality like that I couldn't even fathom not making over six figures let alone being broke. That shit is not even in my vocabulary.

Work was a complete drag but it gets like that from time to time. My boss, the Marketing President, is stressed about a major proposal coming up, thus, stressing me out. His old ass called me directly seventeen times asking me about progress on our final presentation. 'We'll have it done by end of day' was my response every damn time. Why he couldn't seem to grasp that concept beats me.

I didn't have time to go on a lunch break today because I was reviewing and submitting proposals. On top of our major design that we had to crank out in less than twelve hours, there were countless other problems; including two of our analysts submitting resignations.

Motherfuckas couldn't take the heat so, they got out the kitchen. Being down two analysts meant that I would have to do some of that work until we could replace them in the next few weeks. I started out as a Marketing Analyst so I was very familiar with the process. Despite my shortcomings, I handled my day-to-day business flawlessly by submitting a final pristine design proposal to the President.

He called me that eighteenth time and said, "I don't know why I ever doubted you."

That's what the fuck I been trying to tell his ass. I don't know how many times I'm going to have to prove myself but, I'm always up for the challenge. I considered that phone call as my pass to go home and I did so shortly after six.

On my way home from work Camille called. "What's good Cam? You must be tryna make a move?" I knew what was up.

"You already know, my nigga. I got this lil move for us. I know how you don't really like blind dates and all—"

"Hell naw!" I interrupted before she could even get the sentence out.

"Damn! Just listen. Tony's homeboy from Atlanta is in town and he has tickets for us to go to the Summer Music

Jam. And I know you been wanting to go to this concert."
Tony is some random guy that Camille met at her club. I
haven't met him nor do I know anything about him. She has
barely mentioned the guy other than his looks. But, that
was Camille's style. She entertained men for a few months
then, moved on to the next. Now, that I think about it,
Summer Jam tickets for free didn't sound like a bad idea
after all.

"For real, the Summer Jam at South Beach?"

"Exactly, yo boy Sly Hood gone be there," she said
while laughing.

I dated Sly when I was in college for like two years.
Biggest waste of time I've ever experienced, but I was stuck
on hood dudes back in the day. I was into the flashy money,
well known kinda guys but those type were the dogs. And
Sly definitely lived up to that stereotype.

"I guess I'll go. I ain't got nothin' better to do." I
ignored her comment about Sly.

"Cool. We'll pick you up at eight."

Camille's ass rushed me off the phone before I
could change my mind. She just better hope this guy she is
trying to set me up with ain't busted. Because I would have
no problems letting dude know that he is not my type.

While on my way home, I'm in the car jamming to my Neo Soul mix when my phone rings again. It was an unknown number with an area code that I didn't recognize.

"Taya Roberts, whom am I speaking with," I said very professionally.

"Ms. Taya," a handsome voice responded.

"Who is this?" I had no clue.

"Ken calling you from my hotel room in Boston. "

"Oh, KC. How are you?" I said with this extreme smile on my face.

"I'm doin great. How yo pretty ass doin?"

"I'm doin well. Just wondering when you're coming back to Miami so we can have a second quarter," I said flirtatiously.

He laughed.

"Well, actually, that's why I'm calling you. I wanna fly you out to Oklahoma. You can come see me play then we can hit the club or something after," he offered.

I thought about it briefly. "Hell yea, I'm down."

"Alright, bet. I'll get your ticket for Friday."

I gave him my email address so he could send me my flight confirmation and then we said our goodbyes. By the time I got off the phone with KC I was pulling into my parking spot and walking up to my apartment. It was already 6:30, so I needed hurry up and start getting ready. As I showered, I thought about Mike and the steamy encounter we had the last time we were together. I also thought about how I haven't heard from him all day. *Here he goes again with his piss poor communication skills.* It's cool though because I have other things on my agenda for tonight.

After I got out the shower I got fresh, of course. I'm the type that will always walk out the house looking my best, regardless of the circumstance. I ended up rocking some dark denim True Religion skinnies, a sheer red sleeveless blouse, and some black pumps from Aldo. And, of course, my ass was sitting fat and my twins were present and accounted for. My hair was in a slick, tight ponytail and my face was modestly put on. Before I knew it, Camille was calling my phone telling me to come downstairs.

I walked outside to find an all-black Tahoe sitting on sixes decked out in tint. I couldn't see anybody in the car, but I knew it was them. Nobody in my neighborhood is hood enough to put twenty-six inch rims on their sixty-five thousand dollar SUV. When I got in, Tony was in the driver's seat, his friend was in the passenger seat, and Camille was sitting in the seat behind him.

"Guys, this is my best friend, Taya. Taya this is Tony and Sean." She pointed to everyone as she introduced us.

Though it was kinda dark I can tell that Sean is quite attractive. His best features include caramel flavored skin and nice teeth. He also smelled good and dressed well. This might not be so bad after all. I extended my hand over to him. "Nice to meet you," I said sincerely.

"Camille told me a lot about you," he said as he checked me out. He nodded in approval.

"I'm sure she has," I responded while I looked directly at Camille.

Tony turned up the radio and rapidly pulled off. You know how niggas gotta unnecessarily pull off when they tryna impress somebody. Thirty minutes later we pulled up to South Beach. It was already extremely packed. Luckily Tony had VIP parking passes, so we got to park directly in the front next to a red Dodge Charger.

"This concert is about to crack!" I said.

"I know! Rick Ross, Meek Mill, Wale, and Sly Hood! It's bouta go down," Camille responded, sounding like a damn bopper.

The concert was live, like I predicted. It was packed

to maximum capacity and every artist turned the stage up. Sean was all up on me from behind like I was his girl or something. It was cool though because he is attractive and I was enjoying his company. After the performances we walked backstage to mingle. I immediately saw Sly and he started talking to me off jump; explaining how he living good and how I should come fuck with him. But I been there, done that, and I'm not going back. I hated that we lived in the same city and socialized in the same circles because we always seemed to cross each other's paths every few months. I made it clear that his money and his moderate fame was not about to impress me. Just as we finished the conversation I heard a familiar voice from behind.

"What's good, bro," the voice said.

"Everything is good," Tony said to that familiar voice.

I turned around to see who it was and my heart dropped. Mike's fine ass was standing there holding a conversation with Tony. He was still in his work clothes. Armani slacks finely pressed and a black Polo button down. The memory of him deep stroking me in his shower popped up in my mind. The way he made me moan sent chills up my spine every time I thought about his soft lips touching my neck while he gripped my ass in midair.

"Taya," a voice called breaking my thoughts.

I was so stuck in fantasy land that I almost forgot that I came here with someone, until Sean walked smooth up to me and put his hands around my waist. As soon as he did that Mike looked directly at me, just my luck. He looked fire hot red, his eyebrows tightened up and his whole demeanor changed to hostile, then he walked over to us.

"What's good?" he said to Sean but he was looking at me dead in my face.

"Oh shit! What's up, Money Mike, I ain't seen you in a minute, bro," Sean said as he let go of me to shake his hand.

It looked like he wasn't about to speak to me and I definitely was not having that. "Sean let me talk to Mike alone," I told him as I motioned him to leave. Sean walked off with this puzzled look on his face.

"What's good?" he said, of course.

"Nothin much. Enjoying the concert."

"What you doin here with this nigga?"

"It ain't nothin, I'm just kicking it. You know," said that in my slick voice.

"Oh, alright," he chuckled.

"So what you bouta be doin for the rest of the night?" I asked, trying to change the subject.

As soon as I said that a bad ass chick walked up. She was five-feet two, one-hundred sixty pounds all in her thighs and ass, she was thick as hell. She was rocking a tight ass short grey club dress. She wrapped her arms around him.

I stood there looking stupid as fuck.

"You know," he said with a smile on his face, pointing at the girl.

I rolled my eyes and walked off. Pissed.

I found Camille, Tony, and Sean and told them I was ready to go. I got even more heated when we got back to the car and I saw that red Charger. How could I walk past this car and not recognize it was his? I guess I was so wrapped up in the excitement of the concert that I didn't pay enough attention.

"Damn, fool, what happened?!" Camille yelled at me in the backseat.

"Man, why ain't nobody tell me Mike was gon be there!"

"What you got a problem with my boy?" Tony

asked.

Everybody rambled off something different but I wasn't listening. I was thinking about how I should have slapped that bitch for wrapping her bum ass hands around my dude. Bitch.

When I got back in the house I poured a drink, Henny straight on the rocks. I picked up the phone and called Mike. It rang twice and then it went to voicemail.

11 Mediocre at Best

"Mike where we bouta go," Jasmine asked when we got in the car.

"You about to go home once I get to yo apartment building," I said without even looking over.

"I thought you was gon dick me down tonight," she said while she ran her hand across my dick.

"I don't feel like fucking you tonight. I'm not in the mood." I didn't lie. Taya had me pissed off.

Jasmine whined and pouted the entire car ride while I tuned her horny ass out. All I could think about was what was Taya doing with Sean. Sean is one of them niggas that I know from around the way. Our circles overlap a little but we not tight at all. Matter of fact, it took me a good four minutes to even remember his name before I approached him. I wasn't even really worried bout dude because he not shit like me, but I know how Taya get down. And it didn't help that she was looking good as fuck with another nigga arms wrapped around her. The more I thought about it, the upset I became.

I pulled up to Jasmine's crib twenty minutes after leaving the Summer Jam. She literally tried every trick in her book to get me to pay her attention. I just wasn't focused on her ass.

"Money Mike thanks for dinner and the concert."

I just looked at her while she kissed my ass telling me about how much fun she had and shit. She leaned over to kiss my cheek. Then she ran her lips down my neck while unbuckling my belt with her free hand. Noticing she wasn't about to give up without a fight I put the car in park. She had some big ass soft lips that she managed to run across my entire neck and a part of my chest.

Eventually, I was like fuck it and helped her get my pants down. I reclined my seat back, closed my eyes, and let my stress go while she worked hard to make me bust. She was only alright with her head game but I really ain't the type of nigga to turn down head. Especially, when I didn't have to ask for it. She ran her hand over my shaft while she sucked the head. I hated that technique. To me that is the laziest way to give head. She basically was jacking me off and licking my tip. Trash. I gave in to her horrible head technique and allowed her to lure me up to her apartment since she already had me hard. As soon as I got inside her apartment she pushed me down on the love seat nearest to the door and straddled her legs around me. She is thick as fuck. That ass sat completely right in her short spandex dress but that dress didn't stay on long at all. She went back to sucking me up to get me hard again. I could tell she was thirsty to get fucked but I wasn't really pressed. This is some pussy I already had and frankly it was just alright.

I laid back and allowed her to attempt to swallow my manhood and play with my balls. She is definitely a better dick sucker in the house than in the car. But I still wasn't impressed. When she got me right and was satisfied with his firmness she lured me to her bed, which was close by since she had a studio apartment. Then she lied down and spread her legs as if she was waiting for the favor to be returned. I laughed, grabbed her right leg, then flipped her over to put her in my favorite position: ass up, face down. I definitely wasn't about to eat her out. I wasn't even concerned about how wet she was. She was pressing me for some dick so it was her obligation to get herself wet. I gripped her ass with both my palms and gave it a firm smack then watched it giggle from the vibrations. I pulled out a condom from my pocket, then dropped my pants and draws down around my ankles. I left on my socks and shoes. Even my shirt was still on.

Right before I put it in I looked down to see my

phone lighting up through my jeans. I grabbed it just to check who It was. It was Taya...

12 Taya's Plight

I woke up the next morning before my alarm even went off. I was still pissed about that thick bitch that was hanging all over Mike. I'm mad that he was with her but, I'm more so mad that I care so damn much. I took an hour jog before I got ready for work. I needed to clear my mind and I also needed to reassure myself that I was way badder than that chick he was with. After I ran around my neighborhood in yoga pants and a sports bra, I was thoroughly convinced. From the time I stepped off the elevator of my building until the time I walked back through the front doors every man stared at me like I was a scoop of ice cream on a waffle cone. Yea, I still got it. Don't even know why I doubted myself.

After that run I was feeling empowered, so I put on my red power suit accompanied by my Red Bottoms. I walked into the office looking fully confident, but, yet, still feeling like shit from what happened last night. Out of all the shit that happened, what bothered me the most was my unanswered phone call.

To my surprise, Mike sent me a text around noon.

Mike 12:06pm

We need to talk.

If he wanted to talk then why didn't he answer my phone call last night?

Me 12:09pm

Ok. I'll call you when I get off.

Mike 12:10pm

Naw don't even bother. Just be at my house at 8.

The nerve of him to boss me around after he got caught with another bitch. Mike swears up and down that he doesn't have feelings for other females and that I'm his "Main." None of that shit means anything because I know he still out here fucking around. Even though he was being completely bossy I was already thinking about what I was gonna wear to his house. I had to remember that I did get caught on a date with another dude. We both were in the wrong, but I'm tryna wear an outfit tonight that makes it seem a little less like my fault.

*****

I pulled up to Mike's house at nine. I would've been on time, but I chose to be late just to let him know that he don't run shit. I stepped out my car wearing black leggings, peach push-up tube top, showing my slim midsection, and black sandals. My hair was flowing down my back in a wave curl. I rang the doorbell. Mike opened the door wearing some black Jordan hoop shorts and nothing else. I swear that man knows exactly what he is doing. He didn't even try to impress me, meanwhile, I'm standing here runway ready. And the mere fact that he wasn't concerned with impressing me was impressive in itself.

"So, you just gon stand there? Or you gon come in?" he said with a slight attitude.

"Well, good evening to you, too," I said as I walked in.

He looked at me with the stale face and proceeded to walk to the kitchen. "I cooked you dinner, but since yo ass likes to be fashionably late, it's cold now."

I followed him into the kitchen and leaned up against the counter. "Well, maybe next time you'll inform somebody ahead of time."

"Yea ok," he rolled his eyes.

Mike was tryna act like I was just some regular trick standing in his kitchen but he's a horrible actor.

"Can you go put a shirt on?" I said as if I was really disgusted by his body. When, in actuality, I was already imagining myself all over his sexy ass.

"Can you go put a bra on?" he said as he pointed to my tits.

"Whatever." I walked into the living room with a fake slight attitude.

He followed behind me. "So, let's skip all the bullshit. What's good with you and ol boy?"

"What's up with you and ol girl," I snapped back.

"She some random chick."

"Well, he's some random dude."

"Well, I don't like my girl chillin with some random ass nigga, a lame nigga at that."

"And how do you think I feel about you and ol girl?"

"Regardless, you shouldn't have been hugged up on a nigga that run in my circle."

"I was setup on a blind date. How was I supposed to know you knew him?"

"I know everybody in this fucking city!"

"Well, who am I supposed to date then!"

"Me! What the fuck?" He walked into the dining area. I stood there for a second then followed him. He seemed sensitive about that subject. I didn't want to press that issue any further.

"Did you fuck her?"

He paused. "Naw, I ain't fuck her." He looked like he was telling a bold faced ass lie.

"Don't lie. I saw her ass. I know how much you like hittin' it from the back," I said, rolling my eyes.

"That girl is nobody. Some chick I brought to the concert."

"And you couldn't have brought me?"

"Well, I could have, but since yo ass walked up out of here the other night without even letting a nigga know something, I figured you ain't wanna be bothered."

He sat on the couch with his arms folded. I sat right next to him, separated his fold and made him put his arm around me, even though I could tell he didn't want to.

"I apologize for leaving without saying bye," I said in a really sweet voice with my puppy dog eyes.

"Naw, don't be sweet to me now!" He looked away like a little ass child.

I leaned in and started kissing him on his neck, real slow with the inner part of my lips touching his neck first then slowly sucking until the skin was out of my mouth. He attempted to say some slick shit but he was overpowered by the sensation of my lips on his skin.

"Taya... look..." Mike said while fighting off his moans.

"Yes?" I whispered in his ear and then I ran my

tongue across it.

He grabbed me by my waist and gently pushed me off him. "You can either be my girlfriend or I'm treat you how I treat these hoes," he said in an extremely serious voice.

I sighed and situated myself on the couch. "Michael, I'm not looking to be in a serious relationship right now. I mean, I really like you, but it's really not time for us to be making a real commitment." I thought about all I would have to give up if I committed to him now. No more NBA players, no trip to OKC to chill with Ken. I just wasn't ready for the trade-offs.

"So, basically you just like being a hoe?"

"Excuse me?"

"Taya I've heard about you way before you even showed up at my pool party that day. Yo ass been hoppin on every major basketball and rapper dick that hits Miami."

"Watch your mouth when you're talking to me! I don't hop from dick to dick."

He chuckled. "Yea alright."

"Seriously. I'm out here doing me, treating these niggas the same way they treat us females. Don't get mad at me because you been stickin yo dick in these basic hoes and I've been fuckin millionaires. Only difference between me and you is that I have standards when it comes to fuckin!"

"Regardless if you have standards or not, you're still a hoe."

"Go fuck yourself," I said as I picked up my purse and walked toward the door.

I walked out the door to my car and just before I got in Mike yelled from the door,
"Tell KC I said what's up the next time you see him!" He slammed the door and I sped off.

Breezy Fall

13 Trying Something New

Who knew that what I saw as perfection, standing at six-feet three with amazing chocolate skin and sexy lips, would be the reason I felt like shit the next day. I spent most of my day thinking about how he could have possibly known my past and how he knew I had a relationship with Ken.

On my lunch break, I met up with Camille and Angela at Uncle Julio's Mexican Restaurant.

"So let me get this straight, he called you a hoe dead to your face," Angela exclaimed in disbelief.

"Yes! And he said it with such conviction and certainty like he had personally witnessed me fucking somebody."

"Are you sure he doesn't know somebody you're close to?" Angela asked.

"Girl that don't even matter. Taya what you gon do?" Camille cut her off.

"I'm not gon do shit! Fuck him. He was begging me to be his girl and then the next thing I know he's calling me a hoe. I can't fuck with a nigga that bipolar."

"Taya I don't think you're going to be able to just

forget about him that easy. But, I definitely think you should," Camille said as she sipped her top shelf margarita.

"Honestly, I have no choice at this point. I don't see how we can move forward from here. Plus, I'm going to Oklahoma City tomorrow to spend some time with Ken, so that will take my mind off him for a little while."

We finished our lunch and our margaritas and went back to work. On my way home, I detoured from my usual route driving down 95 and headed to the mall to exchange these shoes I bought the other day. I jammed to some Jill Scott, pretending like I can sing and shit. Jill is my go to when I just need to simply clear my mind. As I'm riding and vibing out of nowhere my tire pressure signal appeared on my dashboard.

"Really?" I said to myself smacking my lips.

I got off at the next exit and pulled in to Quick Trip to put some air in my tire. I looked way too cute to be bending over tending to my car but I sucked it up and put the quarters in the machine. Before I could get to my first tire another car pulled up beside me. This fairly cute dude got out wearing some hoop shorts and a white tee shirt. Not really my type of dude, so I just continued doing what I was doing.

"Let me help you," a voice from behind me said.

I turned around and the regular dude stood dead in my face. I took a step back to get a good look at him then handed him the air hose. He took it out of my hand, checked the tire pressure on all my tires, then proceeded to only add air in my front right tire. After he was finished, he placed the hose back on the holder, looked at me and smiled then started to walk back to his car. This regular guy was cuter than I thought he was. His smile was radiant and his teeth were perfect. He was definitely an athlete and appeared to be pretty young; maybe his early twenties. Plus, he just helped me out without even knowing me.

"Thank you..." I shouted over to him, right before he got in his car.

"Oh, so you do talk?" He asked sarcastically.

I laughed. "Yes, I do." I replied as he walked over to me.

"You're welcome." Then he just stood there looking at me.

"Hi, I'm Taya," I said as I extended my right hand.

He raised his eyebrow as if he was thinking then responded. "Very nice to meet you," he said as he held my hand. He didn't shake it, he just held it all compassionately.

I blushed. "So, what's your name?"

"Rashad."

"Well, Rashad I gotta go. Thanks again," I said as I gently pulled my hand away from his. He proceeded to his car and I was nearly all the way in my car when he suddenly stopped, turned around and shouted, "Go to dinner with me tonight?"

I looked over at him one more time. It was something about him. He wasn't impressive like Mike, but he was fine and his presence was intriguing. He seemed to have his head firmly on his shoulders and was definitely outgoing and forward with his approach. I thought about the offer. It wasn't like I had any plans other than returning those shoes sitting in my backseat. Plus, with the argument Mike and I had the other day I definitely needed someone to take my mind off him. I entered my phone number into his phone and told him to text me with the details, then I got in my car and drove off to finish my errand.

That night I slipped into a red cocktail dress, my signature look. Something red and tight with my entire frame exposed. I wore my hair in sleek long ponytail to show off my collarbone and flawless nude makeup pallet. I scented myself with a casual fragrance, just enough to add additional attraction but not too much. I had no expectations for the night. I simply wanted to enjoy my stress-free night.

Rashad had me meet him at a quaint lounge on his side of town. He reserved a table for us and was there waiting on me when I showed up. *Punctual. I like that.*

"You look amazing," he said, standing up to greet me.

"You too," I replied. He did. He was wearing a tailored black suit, suede loafers, and a gold accent watch. He definitely was way more clean cut than what I saw earlier. *Now that I see he cleans up nicely, I can take that off the list as well.*

"Thank you. Please join me." He pulled out my seat. I smiled at his gesture. *And he's polite. He's 3 for 3!*

The lounge doubled as a restaurant and bar. The ambiance was chill with low dimmed lights, soft music playing in the background, and cozy plush seating for the guests.

"So what's up?" I asked after the waiter took our drink orders.

"I'm over here just enjoying your presence, to be honest." He smiled. His teeth were super cute and white.

"If you don't mind me asking, how old are you?"

"I'm twenty-two. I just graduated from Florida State this past spring. I can tell you were wondering how old I was when I met you earlier. Trust me, I'm a grown ass man." He cleared that up immediately.

I smiled. "I can see that," I flirtatiously added as I sipped my drink.

"I wasn't planning on giving you my number but you were just so polite, which is something that is hard to come by out here," I explained.

"I could tell that as well. That's why I left you alone. I ain't no thirsty ass nigga." I laughed at his sarcasm.

"So what if I just walked out of your life and you never saw me again?"

"That would be what you call destiny. That's life. If I was meant to be sitting here with you enjoying a cocktail and your beauty or if I was meant to be sitting on my couch in some hoop shorts watching *Sports Center,* then it is what it is," he explained.

I admired his life perspectives. He was conversational, articulate, respectful, and handsome, yet his subject matter had depth and substance. He made it entirely too easy to talk to him and every point he made expounded our conversation. He is what you would call a total package.

After we shared a few appetizers and had a few more cocktails our conversation progressed to deep subject matter. We ended up talking about corporate business standards since we both have degrees in business and work for Corporate America.

"But that's just my view point on saving funds for next years' fiscal budget. Your business appetite for risk will always drive your budget. I mean let's be real, those companies that aren't afraid of a little failure seem to spend a decent sized budget and still come out successful," I concluded the debate.

"It makes sense. I have watched those compliance sticklers drive our management crazy implementing new processes just because they're scared that 'five percent chance' could happen," he agreed. Then he finished off his last beer. "Look, I'd hate to cut our night off, but I kinda need to head out. Work in the a.m. You know how that goes."

"I definitely do."

He paid the tab and we headed out toward the parking lot. Rashad subtly grabbed my hand and gently interlaced his fingers between mine as he accompanied me to my car.

"So, do you want to just come stay over at my crib," I hinted.

He looked over at me. "Naw. Honestly, I want to get to know you a little bit better before we chill at the crib late night. No disrespect," he said, raising and kissing my hand.

I was stunned. "None taken. I can respect that."

"I had a great time with you. I'll call you sometime soon or you can hit me up whenever," he smiled.

"Alright cool." I was nonchalant after he rejected me.

Rashad opened the car door and closed it behind me then he made his way to his Chevy Impala and we both dipped. I drove home that night still stunned by Rashad's rejection. This had to be the first time in life a man of any caliber told me he didn't want to go home with me. But his blatant respect for me was uncanny and simply unmatched by any other individual. I definitely will be giving him another call in the near future.

14 Pop Bottles, Fuck Bitches

I woke up feeling better than I did yesterday, but that was probably because I had Rashad on my mind instead of Mike. That was the difference between a man that stimulates your body versus and man that stimulates your mind. It was also a better day because today marked my trip to Oklahoma City and with the added stress at work I was hyped about getting away from Miami for a little bit.

My flight doesn't leave until 2:30 p.m. so, I decided to have a chill morning: yoga, full breakfast, and a bubble bath. I will be the first person to admit that I am not the biggest fitness junkie but I do like to stay in shape so when I have a little free time I like to get in some physical activity. My apartment complex has a full gym and dance studio as amenities. Each Friday morning there is a professional yoga instructor that leads our class. That one-hour session got the blood and sweat flowing. After my bath, I jumped into a long all white maxi skirt and a pink midriff. I was ready for this weekend trip to Oklahoma. I need a break from my demanding job and my inconsistent love life. I dragged my Louis Vuitton luggage downstairs to the parking garage, loaded up the car and made my way to the airport.

*****

I touched down in Oklahoma City and was immediately greeted by a chauffeur. There wasn't much that impressed me about Oklahoma but a vacation is still a vacation no matter where you travel to. I was escorted to the Doubletree and taken up to the top floor to my suite. The bellman dropped my bags off in my all white suite that was covered in white roses. My room was a presidential suite, with brand new plush furniture, marble floors, plush carpet in the bedroom and a fully stocked bar. KC knew my style. There was a note on the table:

I can't wait to see you after the game

- KC

The note was accompanied by an envelope that held a ticket for the basketball game. *Wow. He went all out for me. I didn't know my pussy was that good. Damn.*

I took a long bubble bath in the enormous spa bathtub, did my make-up, and got dressed. I was having a slight wardrobe dilemma. It was either I get super sexy in a cocktail dress or I go with casual sexy in jeans and a tee. *I am going to a basketball game; casual would be best.* I was fitted in dark Levis, gray cotton tie-up midriff tee shirt, and some white Huaraches. I placed my hair in a simple high bun and modest nude makeup. I look good, as usual.

As I walk off the elevator some light skinned chick rushes up to me.

"Are you Taya?" she said somewhat excited.

"Yes?" I hesitated.

"Hi, I'm Erica, Ken's publicist. He asked me to accompany you to the game, so that you won't be alone."

"Oh, ok cool. Actually, that's great. I like to commentate on the game and I don't wanna look crazy talking to myself." We both laughed.

"Cute shoes girl," she said as we walked toward the limo.

"Thanks," I smiled.

We rode over to the arena, Erica took me through the back press entrance that's full of paparazzi. Random people are snapping pictures of me and asking who I was. "Are you a basketball wife?"

"Ignore them, please," Erica said with a grotesque look on her face that expressed her disdain. "They're always fishing for a fucking story."

It's an NBA game so celebrities are flocking around every corner. "Is that Michael Rowland? From that popular ass reality show? Damn he is fine." I let slip out my mouth.

"Don't be a groupie, Taya. There's enough of those running around here." Erica replied.

It's not even in my character to be impressed by a man but there are a few that get to me. Nonetheless, she was right. I am way too tight to be drooling over a man regardless of his status. Michael Rowland should be drooling over me.

We finally made it to our seats in a private skybox overlooking the arena. I'm more than familiar with the skybox lifestyle. I've been around an NBA player or two.

"This is Ken's private skybox for his family and friends. You also have a seat on the floor. But, I always like to watch the game from this angle. Plus, it's more low key," Erica explained.

Erica and I watched the game, drank champagne and commentated on anything we saw. From the phenomenal basketball performance from Ken to all the women working their asses off to get noticed. After the game we attempted to make our way to the breezeway near the locker room. There were thousands of people standing around waiting for the players. Cameramen, news reporters, agents, celebrities, and plenty of women.

"Can we just go? I'll catch Ken later," I said,

frustrated, ready to leave.

"Sounds good to me," Erica replied.

We finally made our way back to the limo. "Let's hit the club!" I said as soon as Erica got in and closed the door.

She laughed. "I'm down! What about Ken?!"

"I'll call him and tell him to meet us out," I replied.

I pulled out my iPhone and scrolled down my contacts. "What's up baby?" He picked up the phone on the first ring.

"Oh nothing. Just out here in YOUR city wondering why I haven't seen you yet," I said flirtatiously.

"I know, man. I'm about to shower and go through therapy and then I have to answer these press questions. And then I'm yours for the rest of the weekend."

"That's cool, I understand you're a busy man. Me and Erica are going out, you should meet up with us."

"Alright that sounds good. Don't be out here with nothin too sexy on. I don't wanna have to beat nobody ass!"

I laughed. "Of course not," I replied sarcastically.

I hung up the phone with Ken.

"Hey Driver! Take me back to the hotel please," I yelled toward the front.

"I thought we were going out?" Erica fired off.

"We are. I just need to change first." It was no way in hell I was going to the club in jeans.

*****

Erica and I walked in Club Fashion in Downtown Oklahoma City looking like two million dollars. Of course, I had to stunt in a black halter romper and some multi colored suede wedges. My ass was pokin' out something serious! We immediately walked over to the bar.

"Let me get a bottle of Ace of Spades!" I yelled over the counter to the bartender.

"GOTDAMM! You fine!!" Some thirsty ass brother commented.

"Thanks," I said with a snotty ass attitude and looked away.

"Don't be like that, sistah! Let me buy ya drink for ya," he replied.

I kinda laughed on the inside because I knew for a fact that this dude didn't have nearly enough money in his wallet to purchase my bottle.

I smiled at him. "Sure, why not."

The bartender came back with the bottle. "That'll be twelve hundred dollars," she said.

I looked over to ol' dude whose mouth was hanging

all the way down to the floor at this point. I reached in my pocketbook and handed her my black card. "I'm outta yo league, boo. Sorry," I said as I patted him on his shoulder.

The bartender handed me my card, I grabbed my bottle, and Erica and I made our way to VIP. Once, we got up there we popped the bottle and got loose.

"You're a wild girl, Taya," Erica said to me as we twerked to 2Chainz.

"I can be at times!"

Just as I said that somebody came up behind me and grabbed me by the waist. I turned around and Ken's super tall ass was staring at me.

"It's about time you showed up!" I yelled at him.

"Man, I know. I was rushing to get to you!" he said as he let his hands roam around my body.

KC pulled me over to a plush love seat that was ducked off in a corner. He poured himself a glass of champagne and put his arm around me.

"You havin' fun?" he asked me.

"Well, it's not like Miami, but I'm enjoying myself so far."

"I'ma show you a good time, don't worry. Matter fact, let's go."

We informed Erica that we were leaving and made our way downstairs. Everybody tried to get Ken's attention even with him holding my hand. Independent media outlets snapped pictures of us from every direction. It was crazy! When we walked out of the club, the valet immediately brought up his all-white Range Rover and we got in.

"So, what are we doing?" I asked promiscuously.

"I'ma give you a little tour of my city," he said confidently.

We drove around talking, laughing, and playing around. We ended up parked overlooking the lake near his neighborhood.

"I got a question," I said to KC.

"What's up baby?" he replied.

"I'm still shocked that you even saved my number in your phone. Why did you fly me all the way out here?"

"I ain't gon even front. When I met you in the club that night, I was just tryin' hit something real quick before we flew back. But, I fuck with you though. You got this real confident demeanor about you, that shit just turns me on. Plus, you got that wet wet."

Ken explained and then he leaned in and started kissing me. I could tell he was infatuated with my lips by the way he sucked on my bottom lip in between each kiss. He slickly slid my seat back and let the back down so he could place himself between my legs. He started kissing my neck. He remembered my spots and took his time getting me wet. He distracted me with his mouth while he used his hands to position me. I don't know how he managed to slip off my romper so quickly, but before I knew it he was sliding his dick inside me. I moaned as he strong thrusted up against my clit. Even though I was on top and he was on the bottom he controlled every motion. His body was so much bigger and stronger than mine which made it easy for him to move me however he liked. He took his time. He enjoyed himself inside me. The windows fogged up as we fucked the night away...

15 Ménage á Trois

I woke up the next morning in a large king sized hotel bed, completely hung over and alone. I consumed about three bottles of champagne last night and my body was definitely feeling the effects. Last night, after KC and I had our freak session in the Range Rover he dropped me off back at the hotel. Even though I wasn't expecting him to take me back to his crib and let me stay over there, I at least thought that he would spend the night with me in the hotel room. Clearly, I assumed wrong.

It was noon and I had to get rid of this headache, so I walked down to the lobby in my silk pajamas. I got off the elevator and walked over to the front desk.

"Do you, by any chance, have some Advil?" I asked the lady behind the counter.

"Sure, one moment." And she walked to the back to grab them for me.

As I stood there waiting, I heard a familiar voice off in the distance. I turned around to see who it was, and to my surprise, I saw KC and some other chick walking off an elevator! I quickly hid behind a column that was close by and peeked around to see what was going on. KC leaned down, gave the girl a kiss, and walked out the front door then the girl got back on the elevator.

"Ma'am! Ma'am!" The lady behind the front desk called to me.

"Oh, thanks!" I said with a fake smile. I grabbed the Advil and went back up to the room.

I paced back and forth in the hotel room. I poured a glass of wine then popped the Advil and followed it with the wine. I don't care how early it was, I needed a drink. As I sipped I had all kinds of thoughts running through my mind. For all I know, Kenneth Clemson has me and numerous other women stashed away in this hotel for his pleasure purposes. Hell naw! I'm Taya Roberts, I don't get played like this. I picked up my phone and scrolled through the call log until I came across Erica's number.

"Good morning," Erica said through her morning breath.

"No, bad morning. I just saw some shit that could possibly fuck my whole weekend up," I abruptly shouted at Erica.

"Whoa, calm down. What are you talking about?"

"How many other girls does Ken have staying at this hotel?" I calmed down while taking another sip of my wine.

Erica went into this long awkward pause. "Erica?!" I snapped at her.

She sighed, "Taya I actually really like you so, I'ma keep it a hundred with you."

"Ok, I'm listening."

"First off, you can't be getting attached to these basketball players, they're all dogs. No matter how they may set you up and make you feel special. That's just all a part of their game—"

"How many other females are staying here besides me!?" I cut Erica off.

"There's a different chick in each wing of the hotel," she shamefully blurted out.

I hung up the phone dead in her face. Ain't this about some shit. The last time I got played I was in college. I've dated all kinds of rappers, athletes, lawyers, doctors, and a lot of them were a thousand times finer than KC. Here I am sitting in Oklahoma fucking City getting the run around. I sat in silence for a moment while thoughts ran through my mind. Then, I came up with a devious ass plan. I called Erica back and apologized for hanging up in her face. After I buttered her up with sap ass apologizes I swindled my way into getting her to tell me the names of the other three girls that were in the hotel.

After I hung up the phone with Erica I immediately called the chick at the front desk and asked for the room numbers of all the girls that Erica listed to me. She gave them to me after I pitched a believable lie to her. I told her I was here on a girls trip and wanted to surprise them with breakfast this morning. I called all the girls individually and filled them in on Ken's game. All of them were as surprised as I was and each of them described the exact same game that was run on me. We all decided to meet up in the lobby in a couple of hours.

"I met KC in New Orleans when they played the Hornets. He had me convinced that he was into me on a deeper level," Janae explained as we sat around a table in the cafe of the hotel. Janae Michaels is an editorial model from New Orleans. She stands about six-feet two with gorgeous brown skin and short, dark, curly hair.

I shook my head in disgust. "This takes tricking to a whole new level."

"How we gon get this sheisty ass fool back?" Kennedy exclaimed in sheer anger. Kennedy Ross is radio personality from Los Angeles who is known for her ability to keep it real and spare no feelings. She's short and thick, heavy sex appeal, light skin, and long brown hair.

"How about we just go home and leave him looking stupid?" Carly suggested. Carly Simon is a powerful criminal law attorney from Michigan. She's somewhat passive when it comes to her personal life, but in the courtroom she is an undeniable force. She's about five-feet six inches and dark skinned. She is also the chick that I initially spotted KC with this morning.

"No, that's way too easy. We gotta make him pay and it has to be good," I said brainstorming. "I got it!" I exclaimed as I pulled out my phone.

"What is it?" Kennedy immediately questioned.

I held my finger up at Kennedy as the phone rang. "Hey, what's up? You busy tonight? Perfect, come to my room around ten. I got a lil surprise for you," I told Ken seductively. Then I hung up.

"What's the plan?" Janae exclaimed anxiously.

"This is what we gone do..."

*****

That night my hotel suite was lit by candle and covered in rose petals and the champagne was on chill. I made sure I was looking bedroom ready in a black lace bra and panty set. Just as I finished putting the last few touches on the room, there was a knock at the door. I walked over to open it.

"Damn, Taya! You went all out for ya boy!" Ken expressed in complete delight.

"Of course, anything for you, KC!" I said in the fakest voice I could find.

I lured him into the room and poured him a glass of champagne, then I straddled him on the bed.

"You must have really missed me," he said as I took off his shirt.

"You have no idea," I flirted.

After I took all his clothes off, I pushed him back on the bed and handcuffed his hands to the headboard.

"You on some freaky ass shit."

I ignored his comment and began to get his dick hard. I slid his dick into my mouth and gripped the tip with my throat. His toes curled instantly. He called my name like he was ready for me. I starred him down while I glossed his entire dick. I ran my fingers over his sack then gripped his shaft as I slid my mouth off. As soon as he was fully erect I got up off the bed. He immediately tried to sit up but, then realized his wrists were restricted by the handcuffs.

"Whoa, where you goin?"

"Oh, I'm not goin anywhere, just thought we needed some more company."

"Some more company?"

As soon as those words left his mouth Janae, Kennedy, and Carly stepped out. We stood there in our lingerie looking like the Victoria Secret version of the Fantastic Four. Ken looked like he was about to shit a brick!

"What's going on?" he said with a shaky voice.

"You tell us!" Carly declared.

Before Ken could even reply Kennedy jumped on the bed and began to tease him. She slid her thick ass and thighs on his chest and spread into a split then she removed her bra and flipped over so that his dick was between her legs.

"You gon get on it?" KC had the audacity to ask.

"Fuck no! You will never feel the wetness of this box ever again!" Kennedy said with tenacity.

Carly, Janae, and Kennedy proceeded to have a threesome directly in front of KC. I sat back and watched from the side. Kennedy sat her pussy on Carly's tongue while she ate out Janae. I could see Ken squirming in those handcuffs as his penis stood tall! Janae started to moan uncontrollably. Kennedy pushed her legs up behind her head and sucked her clit until she creamed then Kennedy slurped up every last bit of it!

"Damn, K. Ross! Is it like that?" I commented from the sideline.

"You wanna find out?" she said with a smile.

Right before I answered Carly distracted her with her tongue. After Kennedy made Carly cum, Janae and Carly rotated between Kennedy's DD bombs and her pussy until she couldn't take the pleasure anymore. When they decided they had enough fun for the night all four of us put on our clothes, grabbed our stuff, and headed out the door.

"Where y'all goin?! Somebody uncuff me!" KC yelled as we shut the door.

As we walked down the hallway we reminisced on what just happened. We figured house keeping would get to Ken in the morning and by then he would have had enough time to think about the damage he caused trying to play us. In the meantime, we took this opportunity to make new friends from an unfortunate situation.

"Are you a lesbian?" Janae asked Kennedy.

"Nope, I'm a nymphomaniac. I love sex in any form or fashion," she replied.

"Well, after that scene all three of y'all are bisexual.

And y'all are quite good at it if I might add," I commented.

"I shoulda turned yo ass out too!" Kennedy stated as she handed me her business card. "Hit me up sometime."

I could have easily joined in on our revenge plot but that's not really my style. Plus, it was way better being the mastermind of the whole situation. We all exchanged numbers and parted ways. I took the first cab available straight to the airport. Miami here I come!

16 Something Old

The whole weekend had passed and I hadn't heard one word from Taya. And I'm pretty sure she would tell anybody that I never hit her up but in reality she never hit me up either. I didn't too much give a fuck anyway because I'm pretty sure I had a good idea where she was. And after the last conversation we had I doubt I'll hear from her any time soon. Today, I was in my office working; planning my next event, when my phone rang.

"What's up," I answered

"Hi, Michael." The voice was familiar but I wasn't a one hundred percent sure who it was.

"What's good? Who is this?"

"Don't play like you don't recognize my voice." The snooty remark had to mean it was only person.

"Danielle. What's up?"

"Oh nothing much just checking in to make sure we are still on for our lunch date?"

"That's today? I hadn't even checked my schedule." I buzzed Taylor.

"Yes, Mr. Keith?" she promptly answered.

"Do I have lunch plans?" There was a brief pause while she checked.

"Yes, sir. A late lunch request for 1:30 p.m. with Ms. Danielle."

"Alright thanks." I picked my cell back up. "So what's the plan, Danielle?" I reintroduced myself to the conversation.

"Oh, nothing special. I reserved a table for us at Chateau De Brazil on Fifth Street. I'll pick you up. Just don't play that Mr. Cool game and try to be ten minutes late," she responded like she just knew me so well.

I laughed a little because she was right. "I'll be ready."

Despite not knowing that I had a lunch date I was still looking pretty dapper if I might say so myself. Straight fitted slacks from Armani Exchange with a nice black button down and some Louboutin loafers. I had just got a fresh cut yesterday afternoon, so I was pretty sure I would match Danielle's standards for our date. Right when I was checking myself out in my full length mirror Taylor peeked into my office.

"What's up, Tay?"

"Oh nothing just checking with you to make sure

you're prepared for your lunch. You seemed a bit startled about the appointment. Shall I pull anything out of the closet and iron for you?"

I was still giving myself a glance over in the mirror. "You think I look good today," I vainly asked.

"Of course, sir, as usual." Taylor bashfully smiled.

"You don't have to lie," I laughed.

"Honestly, I have yet to see your look not up to par. However, I would recommend that you change your belt for a more understated look. The large LV belt buckle just screams 'pay attention to me'. There's a spare black YSL belt in the closet," she suggested.

"Yea, you're right. Let's do that," I said as Taylor walked out the door and promptly returned with the belt. I made that simple change and I must say she was right. I looked good enough to impress an ex. *Cool.*

Danielle was parked out in front of the building in her C class Benz. I grabbed my keys and my phone and walked out my office past Taylor's desk.

"Hold all my calls. I'ma be a tad bit busy for the next couple hours," I told her right before I hopped on the elevator, she gave me the *I already knew that* look.

When I got in the car Danielle was sitting there in

this tiny ass midday dress. Thighs all the way out and her chest was about to pop out the top of her dress. I'm not even going to lie she was looking real lickable. I could have easily taken her back into my office and bent that ass over my desk.

"Michael Keith, looking good as usual," she complimented.

"Yea you're not looking too bad yourself.". I made every attempt to keep our conversation strictly focused on small talk while Danielle wanted to talk about any and everything personal. I'd ask "how is your day going" and she would respond with "good" but then proceed to explain how it's much better now that she's in my presence. Or I'd tell her about some of the things I'm working on at the studio and she'd flip it by saying she wish I'd work on her. She was beyond forward and made it crystal clear that she wanted me. This conversation struggle continued through out the entire drive to our lunch spot.

When we got to the restaurant I did my gentlemanly duty and escorted her inside, opening the doors and pulling out chairs and what not. It was interesting because I didn't think I would ever think about this woman again let alone be on a date with her. It was something different about her this time, she was more elusive and demanding, as if she had something to lose if she didn't impress me. As opposed to the first time we met. Danielle was pretty stuck up and pretentious, which made it hard for me to shoot my shot. But I always fuck with a challenge especially if them titties sitting right.

"Europe was definitely an experience. I wouldn't label it as good or bad, but I did learn a lot about myself during that year or so," she answered when I questioned her move overseas.

"So what brings you back?" I was curious.

"Lots. My family, my friends, new opportunities. You," she said, smiling.

I had to admit that she advanced her game since the last time we were together. She impressed me with even the small things. I ignored her comment about coming back to the States for me because I'm sure that was a bunch of bullshit.

"Just seems like you packed up so quickly and left and now here you are."

"I can agree that the way I left wasn't ideal."

"Shady as fuck," I corrected her.

"This is true." She agreed, grabbing my hands. "But

I just want the chance to prove to you that I know I made a mistake and that I have changed."

"I really ain't too fond of that second chance shit."

"I'm worth it. Trust me." She did that prissy hair flip shit. The shit was kind of cute, but I kept a straight face since she was trying to play me. "Is there anybody in your life at the moment," she curiously asked.

"Actually, I got my eyes on this little prize. She damn near perfect," I rubbed my hands together as I bragged about Taya. Then I remembered I was pissed at her ass.

"Better than me?" She set herself up.

"Well, she hasn't left me, packed her shit, and moved to Europe. So I'm gonna say yeah." She smirked, even though I could tell she didn't like that comment.

Our waiter brought our meals out and placed them in front of us. My plate was sitting right with a fourteen-ounce ribeye cooked medium well accompanied with lobster mashed potatoes and steamed broccoli while Danielle's plate was decorated with a bed of brown rice with a piece of grilled salmon covered in a sweet glaze. We continued our conversation while we devoured our plates. We also managed to get through a bottle and a half of

Cabernet Sauvignon before the bill was brought to the table.

"I'll take care of this," Danielle said as she reached for the bill.

I quickly snatched it out of her hand before she had a chance to open it. "I appreciate the gesture but I got this." I didn't even look at the total I simply placed my black card in the small card pocket inside the bill booklet and handed it to our server.

"Same, Michael. Refuses to let his woman pay for anything." She smiled.

"Correction. You're not my woman but you are my lunch date who just happens to have a pretty nice pair of titties that I been staring at all afternoon. The least I could do is pay the bill."

She laughed, obviously flattered. The server brought back my card and I dropped a few twenties on the table then we left.

"So, Michael where am I taking you? Home?" she asked once we got in the car as if she hoped I would say yes.

"Nah, back to the office. I got work to do, baby."

"When should I schedule our next date? Tonight maybe?" Once again she tried it.

"I got an event I'll be at tonight and I already have a date. You can contact Taylor when you're ready for our next meeting."

Her face turned sour in seconds but she replied, "Fine. I will. I'm determined."

Once we got back to the office I reach over and gave her a hug. "Whenever we do meet back up, make sure you wear that again." I smiled then got out and closed the door behind me.

17 Real

I took the next available flight out of Oklahoma City; I didn't care what time it departed. I arrived back in Miami around three in the morning on Sunday. I was beyond tired and all I wanted to do was spend the rest of the day wrapped up in my covers on my California King.

The drive from the airport to my apartment was dull and drab until "I Used to Love Him" by Lauryn Hill started playing on my radio. Out of all the companionship I've had lately the only person that came to mind was Michael Keith. In the last three days he hasn't called, texted, emailed, or even tweeted me. As much as I want to forget him, his handsome almost impeccable figure keeps floating through my mind. And after the weekend I had I could use a dose of his caring affection to balance my mood. Right as I was thinking about him I was approaching the highway that leads me directly to his house. I followed my impulse and took the highway.

I pulled up to Mike's house a little after three in the morning. The only cars that were in the driveway were his two cars, which was a good sign. The house was completely dark except for his office on the second floor where the light shined through the window. I was nervous as hell and didn't know what kind of reaction to expect from him. I parked my car behind his and hopped out. I was looking so regular in my black and white PINK sweatpants and matching hoodie, with my hair in a ponytail and no makeup.

I rang the doorbell then waited for what seemed like an eternity for him to come answer. The sounds of the door unlocking made the hairs on my arm stand. Mike opened the door wearing basketball shorts and no shirt, as usual. He looked shocked.

"Hi, Michael." Those were the only words I could think of as I stood there looking pitiful.

He stepped to the side to let me walk in and shut the door behind us. He didn't say anything as I followed him up the stairs to his office. His house was cold from the air conditioner. Every room and hallway was dark except for the accent lights that lit the stairwell. He sat down at his desk and I sat on the couch that faced it. For a home office, Mike's was pretty large. His grand glass desk sat against the far rear wall centered with bookshelves covering the width of the walls in the room. There were plush chairs that sat right in front of his desk for when he had meetings and then there is a nice loveseat that sat on the opposite wall of his desk. I always sat on the loveseat while he worked. Normally, we would have conversations in this setting but he wasn't saying too much of anything at this point.

"So what's been up?" My pitiful attempt to break the ice.

"What you doin here?" He asked as he continued to look at his computer screen.

"Is it a problem that I'm here?" I snapped back.

"If you wanna argue you can go."

"I wanted to see you," I responded innocently.

"You wanted to see me at three in the morning on a Sunday?" He asked while looking around his computer at me.

"It's true. Now answer my question," I demanded.

"No, Taya, it's not a problem that you're here," he said cynically.

"So, you're happy to see me?" I probed at him.

"Naw, I didn't say all that." My whole facial expression changed with that comment. "So where you coming from? Booty call?" Mike asked. He laughed, but he was dead serious.

"I was coming from the airport."

"Where you coming from? I know you didn't have a

business trip over the weekend," he responded immediately.

"I'm coming back from a playoff game," I hesitated to say.

He shook his head. "Thunder game right?" I nodded. "So what the fuck you over here for?" He snapped.

"Why are you cursing at me like this?"

"Because I don't understand you. You fucking with other niggas, giving them all yo time and yo pussy, when you could just be fucking with me. I'm sure that nigga gone either dog you out or already has." I didn't even say anything. He was completely right. "So, you not gone say nothing?"

I sighed. "I don't know what to say. Everything you're saying is true." Once again I had let the idea of a new man take over my current situation, when in reality, I had everything I ever wanted in a man sitting right in front of me. I sat there looking stupid and pitiful. Mike typed away at his desk like I wasn't even there. After a few minutes he finally turned off his computer and walked over to me. He pulled me up off the couch and wrapped his arms around me. I don't know how he knew I needed a hug but his embrace made me feel safe. He didn't force me to tell him about my weekend or where I was and what I was doing specifically. It's like he already knew what happened and knew I didn't want to talk about it.

We went into his room and I sat on his bed while he ran a bath. He made sure to add therapy bath salts and my favorite grapefruit bath gel and then he told me to get in and wash my ass. Then he brought me a glass of wine and left the bathroom while I relaxed.

I slept at his house that night, wrapped up in his arms. We talked about the studio and the marketing firm until he fell asleep and then I followed behind him shortly after. If this is what commitment feels like; protective and caring, then I think I'm ready for it.

18 Caught Up

A couple of weeks went by and surprisingly everything has been going pretty smooth between Taya and I. It feels like she chilled out on some of her activities and we been spending more time together. Things were rocky for a while but after some real conversations with one another we came to an agreement. I compromised and agreed to let her make her own decisions about being in a relationship and she agreed to chill on the nightlife.

I decided to take the day off. I was in the office all night, got a lot of shit done and I had been putting in extra hours over the last couple months getting ready for my next big event. Between Shutdown Studio and dating Taya I was wore out. A break was needed.

I hadn't visited my mom in weeks and because I wasn't trying to get cursed out by her I paid her a visit. I spent most of my Sunday morning over her crib hanging out and giving her the opportunity to ask me a million questions about my life. My mom can be described as an overbearing but caring single strong mother. She raised myself and my older brother to be the successful men we are today but, she does come with a judgmental undertone.

"So what's been going on, Lil Mike?" My aunt asked while we enjoyed brunch on my mother's patio.

"Nothing too wild, I promise," I laughed.

"I don't believe that for one second," my mom added her two unneeded cents.

"You always talking bad about me," I responded.

"Cause you know how you are. You need some Jesus in yo life! More often than once every couple months now, Michael Keith." She came down on me hard.

"Can we just enjoy our food? Or you want to continue to explain how I'm a heathen?" I questioned.

"And ya need to get you a wife and stop slutting out all these lil fast ass girls." She chose option two apparently.

"Mom. I told you I'm seeing somebody exclusively," I assured her.

"Well, you ain't brought her around here now have you?" She rolled her neck.

"Can you be patient?"

"I'll be patient when you stop being a playa like ya damn daddy." She cursed like she hadn't just got out of church.

"Now you know he far from his daddy. At least he making some legal money." My aunt jumped in on my side.

I nodded in agreement.

"Yea, if you count exploiting naked women and that crazy rap music they make in that studio as legal money then I guess so. Really should have just went to college like his brother and been a lawyer or something hell," she bitched.

My older brother is a big shot defense attorney in New York. He's so big time that he barely comes back home to visit. Which is why I can't seem to understand why my mother would ever wish I was like him. I've been holding her down strong ever since I was eighteen yet she still finds a reason to complain.

"How many times I gotta tell you I make more money than a lawyer. That Mercedes you ride around in and this house you stay in should tell you that," I fought back.

She didn't say anything after that. I effectively changed the subject and got her into a better mood. We discussed anything that would steer her mind as far away from what I do for a living as possible. For some reason, my mom associated popular culture, rap music and the club life with sinning. I guess I could see where she was coming from but, nothing I did was illegal so I didn't see the problem.

*****

After I had brunch with my mom and my aunt I decided a little turn up was in order. I called up my boy Dre to check and see if we had any power moves for the day. "What's good, my nigga," he answered

"Shit I'm chillin, bro. What's the move for today?"

"I got a few shorties coming through the crib later. I got two for you," he replied.

I thought about his offer. I wasn't really that interested, but I still answered. "Alright, that's cool. I'ma slide on you a lil later."

"Bet," Dre confirmed and we hung up.

I wasn't planning on fucking around on Taya at all. It's just when you hit up your single homeboys their moves usually involved females. Muthafuckas ain't tryna sit around a bunch of penises all day. So I was like why not, might as well get some chill time in. I was simply looking for something to do; preoccupy my mind and my time.

*****

I woke up the next day completely hungover. All I remember was bottle after bottle of Ciroc. I normally fuck with the Henn but Dre got vodka for the bitches. And that's exactly what I felt like the next morning, a little bitch. I managed to get cleaned up and dressed but my head was still pounding when I walked into my office. Luckily Taylor knew the routine and greeted me at my desk with the painkillers.

"Another long night, Mr. Keith," she rhetorically asked.

"What's on my schedule for today?"

"Plenty. You have a meeting in one hour with the Miami Nightclub Board regarding your nightclub venture. You can find your notes for that meeting on the homepage of your iPad." She pointed as she spoke. "Promptly after that, you have a meeting with the studio staff downstairs, usual content. I'm sure you know the drill. And you are double booked for lunch today."

"Double booked? How?"

"Well, Ms. Danielle was already scheduled for lunch today at Stuey's Grill on Sixth Street. But Ms. Roberts called and requested lunch. And per your instructions, she is to always make your calendar as she requests." She smiled.

I sat back in the chair holding my head. "I'll cancel with Danielle. Get her on line one for me please."

"Yes sure. No problem." Taylor stated as she walked out to fulfill my request.

I picked up the phone as it rang.

"Mikey. What a pleasure to get a call from you this morning."

"Won't be so much of a pleasure after I tell you I have to cancel our lunch. Important business came up." I got straight to the point.

"Aw and I was looking so forward to wearing this near skin tight dress I just bought for you." I sat back licking my lips, listening to her describe how that dress fit her every curve. "Yea, we'll have to postpone that."

"Fine. Let me guess, I'll need to get with your assistant to reschedule." She sounded irritated.

"Glad you know the deal. I'll be in touch." Then I hung up.

Later that afternoon at lunch with Taya I'm sitting at our usual table at Frenchie's waiting for her. She's always late. She takes that whole grand entrance thing so serious. She literally thinks that showing up on time makes her look less important. Meanwhile, I'm just trying to have lunch and couldn't care any less about her ego. After another ten minutes she walks in dressed in a fitted tan Ralph Lauren suit. I fucking love it when she wore professional attire. I greet her then pull out her chair. She looked mad. But I don't remember doing anything she needed to bitch about.

"I take it you haven't checked your text messages in a while."

"I didn't see you text me, baby," I said, pulling out my phone.

"No. Not from me. I got a message last night from your phone. A picture of some chick in her bra and panties." She calmly spoke with a disenchanted tone followed by a smile. I just looked down into my phone. Then I saw the picture. "Yea, apparently her name is Michelle and let me make sure I quote this correctly," she cleared her throat, "she plans on 'taking my man'." She read then looked up at me.

"Baby... umm..." I wasn't prepared.

"Didn't have enough time to think of a lie huh?"

"Nah, that's not it –" she cut me off.

"The bitch apparently saved my number and has been playing on my phone ever since last night. Explain yourself."

"It's nothing baby. I was just kicking it with Dre and some of his people last night."

"It's nothing? That bitch titties are in your phone and she is coming at me about taking my spot but it's nothing." She got louder.

"Look you taking this shit outta context. Chill." I demanded.

I tuned Taya out as she rambled on and threatened my life. *I couldn't have been that drunk to let some loose hoe hold my phone.* I remember going over to Dre's house around seven something. When I got there, there were six females in the living room. Dre and Terry were in the kitchen making drinks. After dapping up my boys, I went in and introduced myself to the ladies. They were a bunch of butter-heads, super fine ass bodies (probably fake) but their faces were barely average. I already knew a few of them and even smashed a couple before. I told Dre to pour me a double and keep em coming. The last thing I remember is getting a lap dance from one of the chicks. Which one? I have no clue, but after that I passed out. A few hours later I woke up on Dre couch. All the girls were gone but Dre and Terry were passed out on the couch with me. I grabbed my keys and my phone off the table and went home.

I came back into the conversation with Taya still ranting about my "aint-shitness" and how I've made a big ass mistake.

19 Handle My Lightweight

"Well explain why the bitch has my fucking phone number?!" I yelled at Mike.

"Shit! I don't fucking know! You tell me, that's yo phone. Just because a female calls you talking about me don't mean I'm fucking her!" He snapped back.

"See, this is exactly where yo player ass gets caught up! You don't even know how to lie. Don't insult my intelligence with that bullshit ass answer!" I said as I grabbed my keys and my purse.

"Where you going, Taya?"

"Away from yo ass before I end up in an orange jumpsuit," I said right before I stormed out.

Mike is full of shit, I thought to myself as I drove down the highway. *Does he really think that I don't know about his hoes and the dirt that he does?* He tells me he loves me over the phone and then goes and lays some other bitch down. Typical ass nigga shit. The funny thing is that I know about all the hoes he fucks. I am well connected in this city and any bitch that even thinks about touching his dick is reported to me, but I hate a man that does sloppy work. If you are going to fuck with these hoes then you need to put in extra work to make sure that these hoes don't talk. And the fact that one of his bitches has been playing on my phone like a little sixteen year old girl is not cool with me. This bitch got the game completely fucked up. I picked up my phone and called Camille.

"What's good, T?" She answered.

"I got a slight issue. I need to check a bitch and I need to do the shit ASAP."

"Shit, just tell me what I need to do."

"You know some girl named Michelle? I don't have a last name, but I got her phone number. She has an ATL area code."

"Michelle??" Camille was silent for a minute. "I know there's a Michelle that works at KOD, she's a bartender. She kinda short and thick, ugly in the face though. And now that I think about it she did just move down here from Atlanta."

"Sounds like a bust down to me. Can you find out if she works tonight?"

"I'm on it. I'ma call my homeboy that does security for KOD."

"Bet. If she's working, then that's our move for tonight."

I went to the crib and popped open a bottle of Moscato to ease my mind. Then, I waited for Camille to confirm my request. I was too ready to pop off; all I need is the green light. I sipped my Moscato and let my mind replay all the fucked up shit I been through with Mike. I hate that he has this hold on me. The list of negative shit that he brings into my life is about three times longer than the positive, but why do I keep this trife ass nigga? Truth is the dick is traumatizing, shit is beyond good. And what that mouth do? That is an understatement. And on top of all that shit I love him. It's clear he has the same feelings but he hoes around.

Apparently, I love a hood, shiesty, trife ass nigga with a good stroke game. Despite the fact that I am the baddest female I know, one of the smartest and most successful young women in the city. Some shit is going to have to change and it's going to have to change fast.

Just as I was thinking of what my next move is going to be, my phone rang.

"What's up, Camille?"

"We got action. She works from eight to three tonight."

"Cool. I'll meet you at your house at ten."

"Should I wear my Jay's or my Timbs?" Camille asked all extra eager.

"Neither. You can get cute like you going to the club. This ain't got nothing to do with you," I answered.

"Bitch please. I'll wear the Timbs. See you at ten."

****

Around eleven o'clock that night Camille and I pulled up to KOD Gentleman's Club and valeted my truck. We made our way to the front door. I had on some leggings, a Diamond Supply crewneck, some Ray Bans, and some thigh-high stiletto slouch boots. Camille was rocking a short black maxi dress and, of course, her Timbs!

"How you suppose to beat a bitch ass in stilettos, Taya? See this why yo ass need me. I'ma handle up on the bitch for you. She ain't even ready for these hands..." Camille rambled on and on. I didn't even reply.

Once we got inside the club I scanned the scene. Camille tapped me and pointed out the chick to me. "Should I go over there and hold her down while you slap her? Then we can switch?" Camille asked with a serious ass face.

"No, Camille. Just chill. Matter of fact, do me a favor...," I handed her a twenty. "Here, go get you a couple of drinks and just chill. I gotta make sure this the right girl."

Camille walked off to grabbed a waitress and a table. I walked over to the bar casually. I sat down in Michelle's section and waited for her to come serve me. I knew I had the right girl because when she finally got around to me and she looked in my eyes, you would have sworn she saw a ghost. Camille was right, she was a short little dog face looking bitch but her ass sat directly on top of her back.

"Ummm... what can I get you?" She asked timidly.

"Glass of Moscato, room temp," I told her with a scowl on my pretty face. She grabbed my Moscato and then tried to place it on the table and walk away real fast. "Excuse me," I snapped at her. She turned around. "That's rude to not speak to the female that you been harassing all week."

She took a deep breath. "Look I don't need you fucking with me at my job," she answered.

"I don't give a fuck about your minimum wage ass job. I'm just here to let you know something." I took a sip of my wine. "Bitches like you fuck up the game for these niggas. I'm Mike's girl. As in, he cares about how I feel and doesn't need you trying to fuck with my head. You are a hoe. A simple ass bitch that sucks dick when a nigga's girl is out of town. You mean less to him than a one-dollar bill. Don't ever bring yo mess around me or my man again. Or I promise you, you will lose yo job and all yo front teeth." I took a final sip, dropped a twenty-dollar bill on the bar and walked away. "Bitch."

*****

I lay in my bed that night pissed as fuck. Watching my phone ring endlessly as Mike tried to get my attention to preach his sob story to me. I am not in the mood for his lies. The hardest part about being me is that nobody ever knows what I really go through. Everybody sees this super confident woman who can have pretty much anything she wants. But, that is the furthest thing from the truth. In actuality, I don't have anything. Sure, physically I have material things: luxury cars, designer clothes, expensive handbags but I spend most of my nights alone. I have love, but it's untamed and inconsistent. And, quite frankly, that's not what I want or need. I needed closure and I needed to know where Mike and I stood.

As those thoughts developed in my mind, keeping me awake, I decided to make a trip to Mike's house.

20 Uncontrollable Emotions

That night Taya came by, barging into my crib, searching for some leftover reminisce from another female. And of course she didn't find shit. I always make sure my hoes take all their shit with them when I politely kick em out.

"So what? You just fucked the bitch and she left" She asked but I knew she didn't want to know the answer. Honestly, I didn't really even know what she was referring to. It felt like she just wanted to start some shit.

"That's why you came over? To make sure I wasn't fucking?"

"I went to that strip club to see that girl, Michelle. According to her it was more than a few text messages. So what's really going on Mike?" she yelled.

"She Some random ass bitch. Why the fuck does it matter?"

"Did you fuck her?" She asked. I laughed. Then she hit me in my chest.

"Did you fuck her?!" she asked again and stared at me with the most serious face.

I was taken aback by her decision to get physical with me. We had our fair share of arguments every now and then but one thing that I always admired about Taya was her ability to stay somewhat calm. She was different this time. I could tell her emotions were into it and that somehow I had graduated from just "a man she's fucking" to "a man she cared for". I liked her new found emotion and wanted to further explore it.

"Not tonight" I answered her question just to see what kind of reaction I could get out of her. I also didn't want to tell a bold face lie.

Her face grew with tension. She grabbed her purse off the floor at which she threw when she walked through the door. Then stormed toward the front door. I grabbed her before she could get even halfway close to leaving.

"Let me go Mike" She said as she tried to calm herself.

I picked her crybaby ass up as she resisted, trying to get loose and I took her to my bedroom. "Put me down" she yelled but I ignored her request. When I got to the room I sat on the bed still holding her in my arms making her straddle me. I then started to kiss her neck and at first she resisted but once I ran my fingers over her nipples while simultaneously running my tongue against her nape she calmed. Dropping her purse on to the floor and letting her body relax in my arms. I unbuttoned her shirt allowing her to slide out of it then I smoothly unhooked her bra and threw it across the room. I didn't speak. I just sucked and licked every inch of her. I started at the neck softly kissing then I laid her on the bed, making her body completely vulnerable to me, and continued to kiss down her body. Making sure to stop at her nipples; as I played with them with my tongue I listened to her moan. I firmly pressed my tongue against her areola and rapidly making an upward motion leaving her nipples erect and moist. She dug her nails into my arms trying hard not to say my name. I left her perfect breasts and continued my journey kissing my way down to the prize. I slipped her maxi skirt off in one motion and pulled her thong to the side while I slipped my tongue in between her lips greeting her clit. Her back arched as she gripped the sheets. I was playing dirty, flicking her clit back in forth with my tongue until she started to drip. Then I sucked up all her juices by pressing my soft lips against her inner lips and eating it all up. She yelled my name then wrapped her fingers around the back of my head and held me down. I broke loose from her grip

and stood up, unbuckling my belt. I thought to myself "yes
that head comes with dick too" then I smiled at her as she
watched me disrobe. I took off my shirt and exposed my
chiseled body then I dropped my pants and my boxers. My
dick was standing tall. I didn't even bother looking for a
condom. I grabbed her by the legs and slide her to the
edge of the bed and inserted myself. I placed the tip in
first then I grabbed her by the titties and pulled myself all
the way in. Taya was wet as fuck. I slide in and out of that
thang like it was a water park. The shit felt so good; I had
to slow my stroke just to stop from busting. I pulled out
and flipped her thick ass over. Nothing but pretty fat ass in
my face with her head buried in the bed. I grabbed her
waist and guided my way back in. Her ass bounced every
time I stroked and that sight alone drove me crazy.
Watching her brown thick ass bounce when I went in and
looking at that pretty pink pussy every time I came out.
Fuck! I couldn't take it no more. I fucked her thick ass until
I was ready to pop. I pulled out and busted all over that
ass. We both moaned as she left all her cum on my dick
and all my cum was on her ass.

After we showered and got fresh we laid in the bed together in the dark staring out the window at the city.

"Why'd you do that?" she asked.

"Make you cum?" I joked. She laughed then playfully hit me on my chest with the back of her hand.

"No. Have sex with me when I'm mad at you." She clarified.

"I mean... that's the only way you listen to me is if I got you ass naked. Plus, that shit turn me on when you get all jealous and shit with yo sexy ass." She smiled. I knew she liked when I put her in her place. That's one of the main reasons why she fucks with me.

"Why do you keep entertaining these hoes?"

"Same reason why you keep entertaining these niggas. You act like you ready to be serious but you not ready to give up the nightlife. You love the fact that these celebrity dudes throw themselves and their money at you."

"It's not that I love it, I'm just used to living this lifestyle." she replied.

"Yea I know. And unfortunately I can't change your mindset. You have to change that." She looked at me then she looked back towards the window. My arms were still wrapped around her with her ass pressed against me. She held me back.

"You know I love you right?" I told her. She didn't look at me but I could feel her smiling.

"I love you too." She responded then I kissed the side of her face and we fell asleep.

Early Winter

21 Change It Up

I woke up this morning feeling a bit offset maybe because Taya left midway through the night. Or it could be the fact that it was Monday morning and I didn't want to deal with these early meetings or the fact that I hadn't had an off day in almost a month. Either way I planned on fixing both. I normally try to get to the office as early as possible, but today I wasn't feeling it. I scrolled through my phone while I lay in the bed looking at pictures Taya sent me. Though I feel like we made up, I think we left a few things up in the air. I'm pretty sure she's still concerned about my commitment to her and I have some of the same questions.

I called Taylor.

"Good Morning, Mr. Keith."

"What's up, Taylor?"

"Nothing much, on my way to grab your morning coffee. I'll be at the office by six. Is there anything you need?"

"Skip the coffee. Can we reschedule all my meetings today? I'm not feeling it."

"Not feeling too well today? Should I stop by the drug store and grab some medicine?" She sounded concerned.

"Naw I'm not sick, just don't feel like working."

She paused. "This is not like you. But, sure, I can rearrange your schedule this week."

"You're perfect. Also, let's not go into the office today. Matter fact, just come over here once you finish with my schedule."

"Sure" Taylor replied. She seemed confused.

I had my mind set on some activities; one of which was shopping. There were a few items I wanted plus, I felt like blowing some cash. I got up took a shit, showered, then shaved. I got fitted for the day then made breakfast while I waited for Taylor.

When I opened the door for Taylor I barely recognized her. She normally comes to the office in a business casual dress or slacks. But instead, she was standing on my doorstep in some ripped jeans, looked like they were from Express, and a white fitted tee shirt. I never really noticed her slim frame but she was somewhat ripped like an athlete.

"I went home and changed since we weren't going to be in the office today," she explained once she noticed me observing her fit.

"Naw, you good... you look cute," I told her while I let her inside.

Once we ate all the scrambled eggs and bacon I cooked we got in my Charger and dipped. Taylor helped me shop; picking out casual outfits she thought I'd look good in. She has pretty good taste when it comes to men's apparel. While we shopped we chatted about our next major event.

"So, Mr. Keith—"

"Mike. You gotta call me Mike when we just chillin like this." I said, giving her this playful nudge.

She smiled. "Ok, Mike." She enunciated. "How're your plans going for this huge winter event you're planning?"

"Shit gone be dope," I simply replied.

"As usual, but who's on this guest list?"

"Same folks. All the A list and B list celebrities plus everybody I fuck with," I answered.

"So I take that you're extending an invite to Taya and Danielle," she mumbled, looking away.

"Damn," I said, shocked. "I didn't even think about that."

"Yea. I know you haven't. Can I offer my opinion?"

"Might as well since you're already being nosey."

She laughed. "I just think you're playing with fire. Taya is the woman of your dreams, yet you've been entertaining Danielle. Not that I haven't noticed Danielle completely throwing herself at you. I just think you're allowing yourself to become a little too vulnerable."

I looked at Taylor as she spoke; noticing her accuracy with the statement. "I never really thought about it like that. Taya, that's my baby. Danielle is simply just some play pussy that I'm fucking with at the moment, nothing more."

"And you don't think Taya will have a problem with you playing?" She knew the answer to her question.

"The thing about Taya is she wants to be exclusive but isn't ready to be officially in relationship. So until then I'll keep playin."

Taylor looked at me like she was dropping the subject and we continued shopping. "Well, let me get back into secretary mode." She cleared her throat and gave me a slick grin. "Mr. Keith, you have dinner plans tonight with Ms. Danielle nine o'clock sharp."

"Cool, cool. Before I do that let's stop at this jewelry store. I feel like being generous and getting something for my baby."

"Just to be clear, we are talking about Taya right?" She tried to be funny. I shot her a sharp look.

We stopped by Premium Jewelry, where I get all my diamonds and chopped it up with my favorite jeweler.

"Money Mike. What's up, my brother?" My boy Dame dapped me up.

"Same ol', my dude. Just tryna spend some cash with you."

"That's exactly what I like to here. What can I help you with?"

"I need some ice for my baby. Something dope."

"Hmm…" he thought for a second. "You know what… I just cut this flawless stone princess style this morning. If she's your baby like you claim she would appreciate a nice promise ring." He went to the back to grab the piece.

I looked over at Taylor. She looked back with her eyebrows raised. Dame brought back this flawless white princess cut diamond and offered me a hell of a deal on it. I had to take it.

*****

Later that night, I honored my schedule and prepared for my date with Danielle. As I got dressed in a smooth charcoal Gucci suit I thought about what Taylor said earlier but I truly felt like I was just simply being cordial. I mean, Taya knows I entertain random females from time to time. *I think, anyway.*

I sat at the dinner table across from Danielle literally watching her talk her ass off. She went on and on about her plans for the next couple months and where she was planning on being career wise, which was cool and all, but the only thing I could seem to focus on was how nice her body looks in that dress. Then, my mind did that thing it does where it imagines me fucking another man's bitch up against a shower wall.

"You know what I mean?" Danielle took a break from talking to get my opinion.

"Yea, yea, I feel you," I lied. I didn't even have a clue as to what I was supposed to be agreeing to.

"I knew you would," she smiled and leaned over the table, all alluring and shit.

"Look, I got a better idea for us. Let's go back to my crib and finish our convo there. I ain't feelin this restaurant thing right now," I offered.

"I thought you'd never ask, Michael," she replied with a look of relief across her face.

We got in my Benz and drove across town back to my crib. The whole time Danielle had her hands all over me, rubbing the back of my neck and playing with my ears. She remembered all my spots and managed to put her fingers on all of them just to get my blood flowing.

Once I pulled into the driveway, I immediately put the car in park and hopped out. Danielle followed suit. After I got the door unlocked and took off my jacket I picked Danielle up by her thighs and laid her across my loveseat in the living room. At this point I wasn't even thinking, there was one thing on my mind and I was about to check that off the list. She moaned and called my name while I sucked on her titties and played with her pussy. Them titties tasted just like I imagined they would but that pussy felt a little loose. Either way, I was still about to pipe her ass down. I pulled out my dick and put the rubber on, then I flipped Danielle's thick ass over, ass up face down with her stomach straddling the back of the couch. Just when I got my dick in and started stroking the doorbell rang...

22 Impatiently Waiting

The last time I saw Mike he left me with something to think about. He was acting out, proving to me that without us placing guardrails around our relationship he would act as he wanted. I thought maybe I should give up my fast paced lifestyle for a more stable relationship. A relationship with someone that obviously cares about me and has my best interests at heart. That night after I got off work I stopped by the store and picked up a bottle of our preferred Cabernet and some groceries so I could cook dinner for him. I figured it was time I tell him I'm ready for what he had been preaching to me all along.

I went home first to change out of my business professional attire and put on something a bit more comfortable and sexy. Then I made that thirty-minute drive to his place. When I pulled up I noticed both his cars were there and there weren't any other cars in the driveway, which was a good sign, meaning we could have our quality time alone. I parked my car behind his and stepped out confidently. When I got to the door I rang the doorbell...and I waited...and waited. *Where was he?*

I was pretty sure he was home. I could see the lights

shining through the window and I could hear footsteps. I stepped over to his living room window and peered through the blinds. I couldn't see much but I was sure he was in there. I went back to the door and starting knocking instead of ringing the doorbell. Then I waited... *What the fuck?* What seemed like many minutes later, I finally heard him come toward the door. I could hear the door chain click and the locks unlock. Mike barely opened the door and poked his head out the side peeping over the door chain.

"Umm...are you going to let me in?" I asked with attitude.

He looked back and then he unhooked the chain. He didn't even open the door, I had to push it open myself.

"Michael what the fuck is your issue?" I asked as I walked in the door noticing he was standing in his boxers. Then I looked over at the couch and a woman was sitting down attempting to gather herself. My whole attitude went from confused as fuck to savage mode. I walked into the living room to make sure I wasn't tripping. That's when I noticed that the half naked bitch sitting on Mike's couch was Danielle.

"Aw hell naw. Are y'all fucking serious right now?!"

"Taya chill..." Mike started talking but I completely

tuned him out. I blacked out. Danielle was sitting there looking like she was unbothered and that's what bothered me the most.

"Bitch are you really in here fucking my man?"

"He's really not yours if I'm fucking him," she said with an evil smile across her face. "He's too much man for you anyway." She had the nerve.

She took her time putting her underclothes back on like she was in no rush at all. But, what she didn't know was that she played herself because I was about to tag her butt naked ass.

All in one motion, I took off my four and a half inch black suede stiletto pump and charged toward her face. I busted that bitch in the head with the heel of my shoe making sure I hit her ass every time. She squealed yelling for Mike to help. Mike came over and grabbed me or at least he attempted to. I turned around and started swinging at his ass with my Louboutin. I heard them yelling and screaming but I didn't give a fuck. I wasn't stopping until I saw blood. After taking a few blows, Mike was finally able to get his arms around me. I hollered, commanding him to let me go as he carried me away from the living room into the kitchen.

"Get out!" he yelled at Danielle, who was rushing to get her clothes this time.

Danielle, crying and wiping blood from her face, grabbed her leftover shit and ran out the door.

"Taya chill the fuck out!"

I took a few breaths before I spoke. "You're a piece of shit." His face grew sincere. He knew he fucked up. I got up off the counter that he sat me on and picked my heels up off the floor, one was spotted with blood, and I slipped them on.

"Taya. Don't go. Please don't go, baby." I had never seen Mike beg before this moment.

"Go take yo new bitch to the hospital" I said out of spite then walked out the front door.

When I got outside Danielle was leaned up against Mike's car waiting for him. When she saw me come out her face got ghost. I didn't even say shit to her. I wanted to bust her ass one more time but I didn't. I just walked past that pitiful bitch, got in my car, and left. When I finally came back to reality and my adrenaline stopped rushing I realized what just happened. I was crushed. I cried all the way home.

23 Reality Check

I knew I fucked up. A nigga like me can't say no to some new pussy. But I got caught up fucking some pussy I already had. I shook my head at the thought. That's like trading in a brand new Corvette for an old ass Mustang. Damn near got beat to death with a stiletto over some pussy. The same thing that I claimed didn't run me or my life. Yet I managed to let that shit fuck up a relationship that I was building.

I didn't even feel like myself the next day. I awoke in perfectly good health with every piece of my physical life attached and whole, yet I was empty. The shame I felt ate at my insides, opening this void and pain that I never felt before. When I got out of bed I didn't even turn on my normal playlist. I preferred to prepare for my day in silence. I threw on some clothes not even sure if the colors were matching or all the articles were wrinkle free. As I drove the Charger into work in silence I noticed dried up blood on my passenger seat from when I dropped Danielle off at the hospital. And when I say dropped her off, I literally dropped her off. I pulled up to the emergency entrance of the hospital and told her to get out. I felt serious resentment toward her. Don't get me wrong, I am a man that can take responsibility for his actions, but looking at her reminded me of the temptation I felt and made me want to go back in time to the day she originally walked back into my life and tell her to get her tired ass out of my office.

Once I got to work, Taylor was already sitting at her desk, as usual, with my morning coffee. She followed behind me into my office preparing to read the messages from the day before.

"Good Morning, Mr. Keith. There's lots of messages to review since we weren't in the office yesterday..." She stopped when she saw my face. She sat down. "What happened?"

I shook my head then placed my face into my hands. "She found out." The words muffled through my fingers. Taylor gasped. "You were right. I was making the biggest mistake of my life but because I'm "Money Mike" I thought I could get away with it," I bitched.

Taylor sat there shocked as I unfolded the story to her. I spared no details. I told her about me smashing Danielle from the back when Taya knocked on the door. I told her about Danielle arguing with me about hiding when I begged her to get in a closet. I told her about Taya slicing faces with her heels. I told her everything.

"Mr. Keith I hate to say I told you so, but..." Taylor hesitated.

She was right. "I know I fucked up. I made a stupid play and now I'm paying for it."

"So what now?" Taylor asked. I didn't know. Taylor pulled a chair from the front of my desk and sat right next to me. "Honestly, I don't think you ever wanted her."

"Who? Danielle? Hell naw I never wanted that bitch," I snarled.

"No. Taya."

"Of course I did. What do you mean?" I was surprised.

"Are you sure? Because the Michael Keith I know, when that man wants something, he gets it. You knew she was flying out to OKC a week before she left and instead of stopping her you let her go. You also knew she would be at the Summer Jam with another guy and you still let her go. I've watched you stop millionaires from making investments but you can't seem to stop one woman from living her promiscuous lifestyle? You never wanted her. Stop fooling yourself." She stood and returned her seat back to its original position. "Get yourself together. Your nine o'clock will be here shortly. Notes are on your iPad."

Then she walked out and closed the door behind her.

24 That's A First

It had been several weeks since I had even thought about Rashad, let alone talked to him. He initiated a few text exchanges but I'm a tough person to get a hold of via text. But last night at the club I saw him. I saw him out with some of his boys drinking and partying, having fun. He didn't see me. He looked great: well dressed, happy, and content. I don't know what it was about seeing him but it made me remember our night together and the connection we had.

Sitting in my office in between meetings, I decided to call him. It rang a few times too many and then I hung up. I didn't want to run the risk of looking thirsty. He called back immediately.

"Hey," I answered.

"What's up? Sorry my phone was on silent." He provided an explanation for the missed call.

"Oh it's cool. No big deal." I was nonchalant, trying to make it unnoticeable that I was happy he returned my call.

"How have you been?"

"Pretty good." I lied. "Just checking in on you, it's been a while." I dropped a hint hoping he would catch it.

"I sent you a few texts to check on you. I didn't want to come off too forward and make you uncomfortable."

"We should catch up. Sometime soon."

"I agree. Tonight?" he asked.

"Sounds good."

"I'll text you the details." We concluded our conversation and hung up. There was definitely something obviously different about Rashad. But I also wasn't sure if I was just impressed because I was looking for a rebound or if I'm genuinely interested.

*****

I was excited to meet up with Rashad. After all the pointless encounters I've had in the last few months I definitely could use a genuine man in my life. I dressed modestly in black skinny capri jeans, a fitted black tank, and a maroon fashion blazer.

Tonight Rashad chose to take me to an original African American play titled *Strength,* but first he suggested we meet at a nearby coffee shop.

We greeted each other upon my arrival. He was wearing casual pressed black slacks, a checkered blue and white button down, and complementary cocoa loafers. His shirt fit perfectly enough for me to see his biceps protrude through. His hair was freshly cut and his beard and mustache were lined up perfectly.

"Ms. Taya. It's always a pleasure." He kissed my hand.

"Likewise."

"I almost forgot how stunning you are. Thanks for reminding me." He flashed his pretty smile.

"Well, that's what happens when you neglect me for so long," I countered.

His facial expression changed slightly. "About that..." Nothing ever good follows that. I raised my eyebrows. He continued. "I was going to call you the very next day but..." He paused.

"But what?" I was anxious.

"You familiar with Money Mike?" My insides boiled just from hearing his name. I nodded. "See, that's my boy. Mike and I go way back. He taught me a lot about this business shit. Without him, I wouldn't be where I am." Again I nodded. "I would love to pursue. You are literally perfection to me, but my loyalty to him won't let me do that. I hope you understand."

I understood but I was mad. Once again Mike fucks something up for me. "Mike and I do have some ties. And I understand that you have a better relationship with him," I responded bitterly.

"Don't take it personal."

"So now what?" I asked.

"Really nothing. While you're in whatever relationship you are in with him, regardless of the status, I can't fuck with you. But I did want to take you on a quality date, so please enjoy this play with me," he requested.

I felt so neutral about his decision to discontinue what we started. I definitely was starting to see the value in dating a guy like Rashad but I knew with his morals it wasn't going to be possible. He had loyalty with Mike and that wasn't going to change. I didn't want to tell him the status between Mike and I because that wasn't my place. Plus, I felt that would push him even further away. Knowing that Mike and I are basically at war would caution him to steer clear.

Despite the bad news Rashad dropped on me we had an amazing time at the play. Our chemistry was uncanny and clearly obvious. We vibed about everything from our thoughts on the casting to what snacks we ordered during intermission. A part of me kind of wished I had met him long before I was even introduced to Money Mike.

25 An Interesting Encounter

Tonight I decided to spend the evening at an exclusive lounge downtown. It's the NBA All Star Weekend, which means the city is buzzing. I pulled up to Armin Lounge in my white Range Rover and stepped out in a red strapless cocktail dress. I was dolo tonight. I needed some me time on the scene. I was beyond annoyed with my current relationship and my friends would only pile on the annoyance. My confidence and swag completely took over my body as I handed the valet my keys and walked in the front door, skipping the entire line. No matter how shitty I'm feeling on the inside I never let it affect my appearance. Bitches shot rays of fury at me with their eyes as I walked past them and of course I threw a smug look back. The doorman knew me by name and didn't even attempt to ask for my ID.

"Let me get a private booth in the back," I mentioned to the first waitress I came across. She took my name down and told me she would come get me once it was ready. While I waited, I copped a seat at the bar and ordered a glass of Cabernet Sauvignon. I sipped my wine and scoped the place. It was a typical scene, lots of thirsty hoes trying real hard to get noticed by all the NBA players and all the NBA players trying real hard to find the bad bitches. I stayed low key, as usual, legs crossed and glass in hand as I enjoyed the ambiance and music.

To be real honest, I wanted to get away to get my mind off of Mike. Just when I was ready to slow down my fast paced lifestyle shit got real. I thought Rashad was going to help but that whole idea flopped before I could even get it off the ground. Mike was everywhere. What hurt the most was the fact that I trusted him. I spent the last six months falling in love with him and it took a ten minute fuck to ruin it. Mike is still the same ol' hood businessman who can't seem to let go of all his hoes. And I am still Taya; I am not settling for any bullshit.

"Ms. Roberts, your table is ready." I allowed the waitress to escort me.

My table was amongst all the real baller tables. Some of the Heat players celebrating were to my left. The Indiana Pacers walked in and took the booth right next to mine. And all the old head NBA announcers and commentators gathered around various tables. Not to mention mainstream actresses like Lauren London and her clique, plus some of the usual Miami hip hop moguls, such as Diddy and his clan were in the area. As I walked through the crowd I waved at those I knew and exchanged evil looks with basketball wives. This scene might faze a groupie but to me it was nothing. I took a seat on the large booth and ordered a bottle. I leaned back, crossed my legs, and I watched as girls threw themselves at Heat players a couple tables down from me. I laughed to myself because most likely they will take three to four girls a piece to a hotel room have some fun with them and then go home to their wives and pretend like they love them.

Only about seven minutes passed before random guys got enough courage to come over to my private booth and pitch their lines to me. I shot most of them down, but I entertained a few with small talk and then sent them off. Like I said, I'm not out tonight looking for a hook up, I just want to simply chill and clear my mind.

As soon as I had those thoughts, Lamar Johnson of the Indiana Pacers came over and sat right next to me. He didn't say anything at first; as a matter of fact, he didn't even look at me. He just sat next to me, so close that there wasn't a bit of space between my thigh and his. Lamar is nothing short of handsome. Nearly seven feet, caramel skin complexion, full ass lips and long eyelashes; he's literally perfect.

"Can I help you?" I said with a slight attitude yet in a flirtatious way.

He glanced over at me pretending as if he didn't even know I was sitting there. "Nah, I'm good," he said then he turned his head back around and halfway smiled.

I laughed. I thought his approach was beyond cute and very original. We sat in silence for about thirty more seconds then I broke. "Hi, I'm Taya Roberts," I said to him as I extended my right hand.

He accepted my hand, brought it to his face and kissed it with his soft ass lips. "Lamar Johnson."

I was melting on the inside, but I stayed completely composed as I responded. "Pleasure meeting you, Lamar."

"Are you sure?" he asked as he let my hand go. "I felt unwanted for a second."

"And why is that?"

"Well, I watched you pretty much reject every dude that came to speak to you for the last thirty minutes. I was feeling like you're either bisexual, in a relationship, or didn't want to be bothered."

"Definitely the last one," I replied rapidly with conviction.

"You want me to leave you alone?" he sincerely asked immediately.

"Well, see, I thought I didn't want to be bothered, but it seems that I just needed the right company to keep me entertained," I persuasively responded.

He laughed then proceeded to ask me why I came alone and tons more questions to accompany the first. He was really observant and curious, yet he was careful about which questions he asked and how he asked them. Needless to say, he captivated my attention for the next hour, then he excused himself and continued back to his party.

At this point I was about three glasses into my bottle; so I decided to hit the dance floor. I shook my ass and twerked to some club bangers and mingled on the songs that I didn't like. Before I knew it the club lights came on and it was time to go. I found my waitress and closed my tab then headed to the valet to get my car. Just as the valet pulled my truck up and handed me my keys Lamar came up behind me.

"See, now I'm offended," he said, leaning over my shoulder with his hands around my waist. I looked up at him with this sarcastic concerned face. "So you were just going to leave without telling me bye?"

I looked down, shook my head, and smiled. I was completely flattered. "I apologize," I said in the sincerest voice that I could muster up. "Bye, Lamar."

He shook his head. "Nah, that's not good enough for me."

"Then what do you want?"

"I want a night cap," he said with this smirk on his face.

I took a brief second to think about it. Even though I already knew my answer, I didn't want to appear thirsty. "Let's go," I said as I walked around to the driver's door of my Range.

He looked over at his boys and let them know he would catch up with them later and then hopped into my passenger seat.

We rode all the way back to the West Side suburbs listening to West Coast hip hop that he played from his iPhone. He was trying to put me on game to the music that he liked. We had amazing chemistry, but I didn't get my hopes up. I know better with NBA players, especially the young ones. They just want to have fun. So, that's what I prepared myself for.

We pulled up to my complex forty minutes later and walked up to my apartment. At this point, I was trying to figure out what I wanted to do with him once I got him inside. There are two options: one, I could play with him, flirt a lot, let him get a taste then tell him that I'm not ready for this. Or, two, I could fuck his dick off. Once I got to the door and opened it, I looked up at his tall six-feet nine inch frame and those big pretty lips. I thought about all the pussy he probably gets on a regular basis and how he probably plays women all the time. We went inside; I turned the TV on, offered him something to eat, and got comfortable.

And then...I chose option two.

26 The Rim at Eleven

The next day everything felt surreal. Even though I went to sleep with a handsome athletic man and felt completely secure, I woke up alone. My mind started to wander. *Why am I always putting myself in these situations? Making myself completely available for men to just use me for their own guilty pleasures?* I was starting to get tired of being a hoe. Fucking men simply because of their looks and not taking into account my own feelings. I always put on this super tough act, like I don't need a man, or anyone for that matter, in order to be happy. Quite frankly, last night was one of the many times I allowed myself to be completely vulnerable and condone a stranger to enter my body for some sense of false love.

The truth of the matter was I missed Mike. He is the only man that ever took the time to care before he had sex with me. He is the only man that I can honestly say loves me for more than my physical. But Mike betrayed my trust and I wasn't sure if he even deserved to talk to me again let alone get a second chance.

I just lay in my bed this Saturday morning, watching the sunrise and drinking warm tea. To an outsider my life is absolutely perfect. Penthouse apartment in Miami, making well over six figures. But what are all these material things? I was still questioning the value in my life when my phone rang. I shook back to reality, reached over to my nightstand, and grabbed my phone. It was Camille Face Timing me.

"Hey, Tayaaaaa," Camille greeted me extra perky like it wasn't six in the morning.

"Camille. How'd you know I was awake? I could be laid up with one of my boo thangs for all you know," I responded with a slight attitude.

"But clearly you're not. So cut the motherfucking drama!"

"Whatever." I rolled my eyes

"What NBA player pulled you last night?" She curiously asked.

"How do you even know I got pulled by an NBA player?"

"Because you got that depressed "I just fucked up" look on your face. Those ballers always have me feeling useless the morning after. So who was it?" She probed.

"Lamar Johnson," I answered shamefully.

"Mmmm his sexy young ass. Was it good?"

"It was alright. Dick is dick."

"Did he at least lick on the box?"

I smacked my lips. "Now you know he was not bouta go down low! These stuck up ass hoopers never wanna lick on the cat. And that's exactly why I don't give NO neck! Fuck that."

She laughed. "I feel that." Camille has had her fair share of NBA players.

"But yea what is the move for today?" I changed the subject.

"Lakewood Fashion party on the beach this afternoon. Oh and ya Sly boy is having a kickback later tonight. He hit me up on Twitter and begged me to get you to come. So we're going, bitch!"

"Camille. Seriously? You always bringing up Sly like that nigga is somebody I want to see. Are you trying to get me to get back with him or something!" I snapped back. It was almost like she secretly wanted us back together. But, of all people, she knew how much I didn't need that kind of drama in my life.

"Taya stop being a stuck up snob. The man is connected and knows about all the poppin events. That is all. Let's just go. It's not like I'm asking you to fuck the man."

"Ugh. Fine. You owe me though."

"Whatever you always say that, I'll be in front of your building at noon. Be ready and don't have me waiting."

I went back to sleep for a couple more hours before I got up and started to get ready.

*****

For some reason it always takes me at least two hours to get dressed. That's mostly because I spend at least an hour standing in my closet struggling to find the right combination of clothes to match the vibe I was going for. Today I wanted to go for a sexy sleek look. Kinda like a black on black Panamera so I chose black leather leggings, a sheer black halter top, and four inch black suede stilettos. I had to get a new pair of suede stilettos because my last pair had blood splattered on them. By the time I finish curling my hair it was ten after twelve. I locked my front door and headed to the elevator. As I stood there waiting my phone rang. It was Mike.

I ignored it. Just as I had been doing for the past few weeks. I still didn't want to talk to him. I still couldn't believe he was fucking my so-called fake ass "friend" in his living room.

Mike called again. *What the hell does he want?* I became way too curious just to let this phone keep ringing.

"This is Taya," I answered the phone as I stepped on to the elevator.

"Girl stop playing like you don't know it's me," a deep commanding voice spoke.

"What, Mike?" I snapped at him.

"I was just calling to see how you were doing," he said then he paused. I was smiling and I hated it.

"See this is where you fuck up. You forfeited all your rights to checking up and whatever other things come to mind when you fucked my ex-friend. But, if you must know, I'm fine. I just can't talk right now. I'm busy." I fronted.

He paused before he spoke, making sure his next words were perfect. "Give me an opportunity to explain myself. Just one. After that you can forget I exist."

I thought about it. "Fine. Just one."

"Tonight," he demanded.

"I'm busy tonight," I fired back.

"You're never too busy for the things you want in life. Make time for me. Tonight. The Rim at eleven. I'll be waiting." Then he hung up.

I stared down at the phone as the elevator opened on the first floor. Camille was sitting directly in front of my building. I hopped in the front seat of her Honda.

"Didn't I tell yo ass not to have me waiting? You always taking all damn day to get ready," she bitched.

"Whatever. You see how good I look? Takes time to be perfect. Now drive," I snapped at her.

She mugged me for like three seconds and then she put the car in drive and headed toward the west side. After about fifteen minutes of driving we were in deep conversation about my night with Lamar.

"So, he just approached you?"

"He came and sat right next to me. I pulled his ass," I bragged.

"Damn, and you took him home?"

"Yep, rode his dick right on my living room couch. And then I let him flip me over the head of the couch and fuck me from the back. I damn near had him ready to bust after ten minutes, but he pulled out and switched positions."

"Oh, he didn't wanna cum quick," she stated.

"Right, which was cool with me because his dick was decent." I laughed.

The conversation was coming to a close as we pulled up to the fashion show. Shit, I was damn near runway ready myself; I had my conceited swag all the way on ten.

We walked up to the door and Camille whispered something into the doorman's ear and he slid to the side and let us walk through. It was pretty dim in the ballroom, but we were still able to find our seats. I was bored as fuck the entire time. There was nothing but skinny ass models in overly trendsetting clothes. I got to the point of being so unentertained that I started to scan the room for something more interesting. There was nothing and I became increasingly bored with this scene. Out of the corner of my eye I noticed a familiar face. It was Rashad.

I contemplated going over and speaking but then I remembered how he dismissed me. Then he noticed me staring at him. I quickly turned my head. I was not slick at all. He approached me. I started checking my hair and blotting my lips to make sure I looked up to par.

"You don't have to act like you don't know me when you see me." Rashad started the conversation. Then he greeted me by wrapping his hands around my waist for a little more than a friendly hug.

"I just didn't know where we stood. So... my bad." I had no idea why I was nervous.

"Don't be like that, Taya. We are all good. I thought I made that clear to you," he replied.

"I mean after you rejected me I didn't really care too much about the other words you said after that." I laughed to lighten the mood.

"Well you should have cared. I didn't reject you. I paused what we started out of respect. I need you to understand that," he added.

"No, I get it. You made the right call. I'm just being salty."

"Don't. I like sweet Taya so much better." He hugged me and we said our goodbyes.

"Who was that?" Camille asked.

"Nobody really." I was vague. I didn't want to explain the whole story and tell her how I was curved.

I tapped Camille. "Can we go? This is wack." I forced her to be ready and we headed out. On our way to the nearest mall she brought up Mike. "So what's going on with you two?"

"Nothing. After I caught him fucking Danielle I haven't seen him. He called me today inviting me to dinner. I don't know if I'm going."

"I don't think you should." She gave her input. "Fuck him."

"I was already on that. I can't deal with the constant

drama but I did want to give him my final words."

"I guess so. Just as long as your off him then it's whatever," Camille added her disdain and made it clear she didn't like us together.

We ended our day with some shopping. Something that I knew I was good at and couldn't fuck up. For the past few days, I had to mask my emotions and convince myself that I was alright. I didn't want to have to explain to people why I wasn't happy. It was so much easier pretending.

27 The Lighter Topic

I initially didn't even entertain the idea of meeting Mike. But after the thought roamed in my mind all day I decided I owed it to myself to get closure. I wasn't expecting much from our conversation other than him apologizing for his actions and promising he'll never do it again. I'm uninterested in that spiel. I'd rather hear why he thought that shady bitch, Danielle, deserved the honor of sitting on my throne. Even if it was for a midday quickie.

Tonight I dressed modestly. Slim cream slacks, sheer coral blouse, and nude suede pumps. My hair pulled tight into a slick ponytail and a bare face. I wasn't looking to impress him anymore. I didn't need him to be infatuated with me. I wanted my explanation and my chance to tell him how I truly felt about him.

I made myself present at The Rim Bar and Grill downtown promptly at eleven. He was already there. Fully suited in a tailored name brand sport coat and slacks, as if he was about to present in a business meeting. Our greeting was cold. A cordial side hug with minimal emotion or feelings. His face was drab. Still his normal attractive self but it was bland. He had a small cut on his forehead, from our altercation at his home, that seemed to be healing.

"Before we start, I just want you to know the moment you decide to yell, scream, or put your hands on me I'm leaving." He had the audacity to tell me.

Who the hell did he think he was talking to? My face mimicked my thoughts. "I can respect that," I replied crossing my hands over my lap.

We were seated at an open area designed with couches and a small coffee table. I sat directly across from him. His posture was purely professional.

"There's a few things we need to lay down on the table. In order to give both of us the chance to feel closure." I nodded in agreement.

"We can start with the lighter of the conversation topics, Danielle," he commanded.

"That's the lighter of the topics? Your pure cold hearted adultery is the lighter topic?" I was appalled.

"I mean, that's honestly old news to me. That shit happened last month. An unfortunate experience but it's over."

"Oh it's just over because you say it is," I snapped.

"No, it's over because it happened in the past. I got caught fucking my ex. You beat her ass. Nothing else to really discuss."

"How about we discuss why you chose to fuck that slut?"

He laughed. I scowled. "You really need me to explain why I fucked her? Where do you want me to start? With her titties or her ass?" he disbelievingly replied.

"I want you to start with why you preached all that bullshit about us being together then your actions showed otherwise."

"I was gladly ready to call you my girl exclusively, but as I recall, you couldn't seem to get on board with that."

"And that night I was coming over to tell you I was ready," I explained.

"Oh so let me get this straight. Despite my many attempts to get you to be with me I still had to wait until precious Taya Roberts was ready to be cuffed? Fuck my feelings and what I wanted?"

"If I wasn't ready then I wasn't ready."

"But you seemed to be ready for Sean, Ken, and my personal favorite, Lamar. You do know that every time you got slutted out by one of those famous NBA players I received a call the next day with the play by play. I must admit, I'm impressed with how you curved KC in that hotel out in Oklahoma. Everybody loves a ménage. But hearing how Lamar fucked, busted his nut, then dipped on your ass was kinda of sad," he rambled.

My mouth hung low. "When I told yo ass that I knew everybody in this city I meant it. Any nigga you could think of to fuck already got my number saved in their favorites."

"So you spied on me?" I was pissed.

"Hell naw. I got a whole business to run. I have no time to spy on yo ass. I just simply put it out there that I was thinking about cuffing you. And the way the guy code works is that I get reports on your behavior whenever you encounter somebody in my circle. Clearly your little friend circle doesn't work like that." He smiled then sipped his drink.

"You're a fucking snake."

"I gave you the opportunity to be a part of my team. To be exclusively Money Mike's woman. But you'd rather be a hoe."

I sat silent for a few moments. I had to collect my thoughts and push back my emotions. "So what now?"

"Honestly, I don't know what you're going to do. But me, I'm going back to doing all the same shit I was already doing."

"So you didn't come here today to try to get me back." I was curious.

He laughed. And not one of those fake happy laughs he genuinely laughed.

"You thought because you were angry at my crib the other day that I was the one in the wrong? I felt bad that you had to find out the way you did, but regardless, I was gonna have sex with her and frankly any other woman I wanted to."

"See now I'm confused. You can slut around town fucking any bitch with a fat ass but the moment I do it it's a problem."

"The ball was in your court. I was ready to stop when you were ready to stop. But since it was clear you weren't I was prepared to continue my life. You kept going, I kept going."

I scowled. Then downed my entire shot. "I don't know if you noticed or not but you're not going to find a better woman in this city." I found my swag. "I was doing just fine before I met you and I'll be just fine after you." I laughed.

"I think you'll be fine. But from now on when you

go anywhere you'll think about me, wish you were with me, and wonder why you didn't take your chance."

"You just some everyday dick. There will be others." I snapped back.

"Alright cool." He threw his hands up. "So you are okay with me and Camille right?"

My soul dropped. "What do you mean?" I pressed. He paused to take a sip of his drink. That pause felt like an eternity. My mind raced through options.

"Oh she didn't tell you?"

"Tell me what, Michael?" My insides were heating up.

"She's been kicking it at the crib lately. She's been texting and calling telling me about how wrong she thinks you are. She was actually the key moving piece in all the information I got on you. I think I like that kind of loyalty in a female. I might have to keep her." He smiled.

My entire mood changed. I went from feeling somewhat in control to completely losing it. "You bitch!" I stood up and yelled.

"Yep and that's my cue to exit." He grabbed his phone off the table and placed it in his pocket. He took out some twenties and threw them on the table for the bill. He then placed a small box on the table and walked out.

"I'm sure I'll see you around." Then he left the restaurant and my life.

I couldn't believe that backstabbing little bitch Camille. Smiling in my face like she was my friend but the whole time she was plotting on my man. I was boiling on the inside but had to keep some composure because people were looking over at me after my last outburst. After the waitress came by and collected the bill I picked up the small box Mike left. Inside was a perfect hand-cut white diamond settled inside a white gold band. The engraving on the inside read: *What could have been*

28 The Perfect Mate

It took me a few weeks to decide what I wanted to do with myself. After some reflection I noticed that I hadn't been as motivated at work and even on some days I didn't want to go into the office at all. And after Taylor shared her perspective on the whole situation my mind became a lot clearer. Not that I like to blame others for my laziness but I can admit that the issues I experienced with Taya were affecting me.

I told Taya everything. I told her about Danielle, about how I got information on her behavior, I even told her about the secret relationship I had with Camille. Camille fucked with me since day one. I met her at the bar she worked part time bartending where I shared with her the details of my pool party. I told her to get sexy and bring some friends. At that time, I told every woman I ran into the same exact thing. It was mere promotion. When I saw her and Taya at the party I was stunned by her friend.

She acquired my phone number, I'm assuming from one of my many homeboys at the event, and sent me a message about how she was jealous that I was all on Taya and not her. She wanted to keep our "relationship" a secret because she didn't want any problems with Taya. I agreed because I found her quite useful. From that day on I used her to get closer to Taya. She thought she was getting close to me when really I never had intentions of getting to know her like that. She would tell me about the next guy Taya was interested in and even gave me the details of the encounters.

Now that I step back I realize that she was sabotaging me and Taya's relationship the whole time. She was playing us against each other by encouraging Taya to fuck with other dudes. She also strategically placed Danielle back into my life. Danielle confided in her about how she was still feeling me and Camille told her she should pursue. She even gave Danielle the address to my office. She also was instrumental in making sure I saw Taya with Sean at the Summer Jam. The bitch was conniving and deceptive. Taya couldn't see through her own best friend and I was too busy courting her friend.

After I spent a grip on a flawless diamond promise ring that I was going to give to Taya I still couldn't bring myself to accept the conflict that both of us put on each other. In theory, she was perfect. That exceptional business woman balanced with class and intellect and just a splash of hood. But in reality, we clashed. I spent all my time trying to convince myself that I could change her. I became so obsessed with just getting her to be a one-woman show that I forgot the main reasons I wanted her in the first place. We fought each other's natural self, trying to mold a nearly perfect individual into the perfect mate. She refused to let me be the only person in her life and I refused to compromise. That theoretically perfect situation changed into an absolute disaster. Instead of confessing my attraction and compromising for the woman of my dreams, I let her go. Simply because I knew she wasn't ready. I knew she wasn't ready to give up the popularity, the open access to rich famous men. She wasn't ready to give up The Nightlife.

The Coldest of Winter

Shawn Flossy

29 Clear My Mind

I booked a flight to New York City to get away from the stress of the Miami life. Dead in the middle of winter, I step out of the airport to a brisk wind chill and soft white flakes piled on the ground. This was nothing like Miami's everyday perfect seventy-degree weather, but nonetheless, I need a change of atmosphere and some time to just clear my mind.

Spending day after day obsessed with Mike and his limitless options when it came to his love life, is draining. I noticed a change in myself. I became unmotivated to succeed at work and even started to care less about my appearance. I often dreamt about our final conversation and about all the times I had been backstabbed in the process.

I checked into my Double Tree suite located on the top floor on Friday evening and immediately made myself comfortable. I don't know if it was the cool chill of the winter that seemed to humble my mood or if it was the fact that I was thousands of miles away from all of my life's troubles.

That night I found myself at a quaint bar located

just a few minutes away from my hotel room. I was dressed modestly in a red long sleeve sweater dress that came to my knees and some thigh high suede boots. I was seated at a two seat booth in the corner. Usually, when I go out I have all my homegirls with me or I am going on the scene to be noticed, but not tonight. I realized that I didn't have any friends. Danielle was supposed to be my homie from back in the day and she ended up fucking my man. Camille claimed to be my best friend and she was plotting on my man the entire time I was with him. Angela was the only real person that didn't backstab me and I always labeled her a hater. That hater turned out to be the most honest person around me. Either Mike told Camille that he told me about their relationship or she just picked up on it because before I left Miami she called my cell numerous times leaving voicemail after voicemail. I never answered. Mike never called.

I always thought I was untouchable. Infamous at playing these rich men. I thought I was killing the game being a player, but in reality, I was getting played. All these men knew I was an easy target and discussed their encounters with me with each other. I never took any money from them or told any of their business and they got a free fuck. Mike was no different. That night at The Rim I saw in his eyes that he never truly wanted to be with me. He just wanted to see if he could conquer me. Turn a hoe into a housewife. Once he realized how impossible that mission was he gave up and moved on.

*****

That next day after sleeping in well past noon I decided I had wallowed enough in my own self-pity and needed to get back to my usual self. So, I did what has always made me happy. Shop.

I roamed the streets of New York swiping my black card at any boutique that carried my size. Then my phone rang. As I fumbled with my numerous shopping bags to get to my phone, which was buried at the bottom of my purse, I missed the call. It was Rashad. I immediately called back.

"Hello." I was happy to hear from him. It had been way too long since we got a chance to speak and after the roller coaster I called my love life came to screeching halt, followed by a major explosion, I needed some positive vibes.

"Turn around," the masculine voice on the other side of the phone spoke.

I turned around a peered down the street. Rashad

approached me from two doors down in his east coast winter North Face coat. I smiled as I hung up the phone. When he got close enough I embraced his presence with welcoming arms.

"What are you doing here?" I was confused.

He put his arm over my shoulders as we merged in with the everyday city travelers on the sidewalks.

"So," he started. "I went to your office a few days ago looking to surprise you when your assistant informed me you took a couple weeks for vacation. After using my charm, I convinced her to tell me where you went. She gave me the details after a few flashes of my dimples." We both laughed.

"And then..." I probed him.

"And then I sat at home bored all day yesterday. Thinking about you," he admitted.

"And then you teleported to New York?" I joked trying to get him to speed up.

He laughed, sensing my impatience. "Then I took the next flight to New York. I assumed you'd be shopping so here I am."

Rashad and I ended up at authentic Italian restaurant after we literally shopped until we dropped.

"I knew things were a little shaky with y'all but I didn't know it was this bad," Rashad commented on Mike and I.

"Honestly I didn't think things could get much worse after I caught him fucking a mutual acquaintance," I shook my head. "I was so wrong."

"So your best friend was plotting on you your entire relationship?"

"My *ex*-best friend," I clarified.

"That's really not like Mike though. It has to be more to this story," he added.

"I honestly don't give a fuck if there is more or not. I'm done with the drama."

"Well you know there is good news in all this misfortune," he stated.

I looked up from my plate. "And that is?" I was curious.

He smiled then grabbed my hand. "I finally get my chance."

Shawn Flossy

Remember, your enemies are always closer than you think. But, also remember to not get in the way of your own fate. Let your soul guide you to all the right people and all the fake ass people will fall off the ride eventually.

Shawn Flossy

www.ingramcontent.com/pod-product-compliance
Lightning Source LLC
Chambersburg PA
CBHW061453030726
47503CB00005B/1694